D1236160

FANCY

ellipsis
• • •
press

Also by Jeremy M. Davies

Rose Alley

FANCY

Jeremy M. Davies

Portions of this book have appeared in somewhat
different form in *Tarpaulin Sky* and the *Brooklyn Rail*.

Design by Corey Frost & Eugene Lim
Cover art: *Positive/Negative* by Shawn Teseo Ballarin

First Edition
ISBN 978-1-940400-07-5

Ellipsis Press LLC
an imprint of Dzanc Books
P.O. Box 721196
Jackson Heights, NY 11372
www.ellipsispress.com

Library of Congress Cataloging-in-Publication Data

Davies, Jeremy M., 1978-
 Fancy / Jeremy M. Davies. -- First edition.
     pages cm
 ISBN 978-1-940400-07-5 (alk. paper)
 1. Cats--Fiction. 2. Human-animal relationships--Fiction. 3. Pet sitting--Fiction. I. Title.

PS3604.A9537F36 2014
813'.6--dc23
                              2014026079

To Berta Hilde Weidenfeld Zauderer
and
For Sarah, as ever

Perhaps I am doing the moon an injustice.

H. E. Nossack

RUMRILL SAID (FOR THAT WAS HIS NAME): Why not let us settle in with a blunt sort of proclamation, a postulate, for example that this space here, where we sniff and shuffle, is located in my home, Rumrill's home; and that these cats, were any cats present, are my cats, the cats of Rumrill. And then, with all of that said, I might take a breath and illustrate my testimony; I might extend a finger in the direction of my ceiling or walls, at one or another of my little animals—if any had been brave enough to join us—after which demonstration you would be forced to admit, or else persuaded, or else enticed, that I had made myself clear.

He added: Myself, which is to say Rumrill.

Rumrill said: We could then move on to say that you, adrift in my vestibule, or foyer, or in any case where I insist you remove your footwear, where I keep what you won't know is called a "boot-check," and where I hang my umbrellas from pegs—or, rather, my umbrella—that you both, husband and wife, with my front door shut behind you, are here to parlay with myself. You hope to find employment in my house.

He added: As caretakers.

Rumrill said: If we proceed from those principles, which though bare of rhetoric will stand all the more proudly for their simplicity in the deserts of your minds—two bleached barbicans to mark the boundaries of our conversational demesne—we will be able to maneuver more or less freely within their frontiers, so long as the three of us are agreed not to make any attempt to refute them. We may come to complicate them, in time, but must be careful never to remove them from the map entirely.

He added: Otherwise, chaos.

Rumrill said: I am unnerved by your presence here, I'll admit. For one thing because I've gone such a while—though I couldn't put a number to the length of this while—without participation in a single conversation.

He added: Without a single spoken sentence.

Rumrill said: From room to room in my small but admirably provisioned home you might as well imagine my humble, purple-slippered stride, always unaccompanied and always upon the same or similar paths between one room and the next, in perfect silence, or imperfect only inasmuch as it is a perfect human silence, broken naturally by the many sounds of the so-called natural world, which is to say, in this case, the substances from which my house and its furnishings were constructed, once, by sturdier men than

I; and then my cats, whoever built them; and then, really, any part of my own body, save, of course—for our purposes—my vocal chords, tongue, and full, delectable lips. Up and down my single carpeted stairway I would bumble in said silence, up to the one story of my home suspended not especially high in the rank airspace above our town's by-and-large squat, single-storied residences, down again to the ground floor where I cook my rice and brew my tea.

He added: Or, on occasion, "orange-slippered stride."

Rumrill said: I have suffered or enjoyed who knows how long a time with no listener present save my cats—of whom there are twenty, at last count, which count was some time ago, admittedly, but evergreen, I assure you, in my mind—and so no imperative to sift or order whatever words might have slipped out to breadcrumb my trail. The difficulty with speech, I find, when one has fallen out of practice, is not so much that one forgets how to speak as that one loses the knack of thought *at the same time* as speech.

He added: Which trick we take entirely for granted.

Rumrill said: When I've spoken to my many cats, or spoken aloud without any addressee in mind, or without even the intention to speak, of course my cats must hear it. At these times, however, I do not speak to be heard—as I do, I think, now; I am *over*heard, but not listened to, which perhaps means that this activity is not speech at all, but on the order of eructation.

He added: In the final analysis.

Rumrill said: To whom, I wonder, in operas, are

the arias addressed? The unimaginative would say, "to the audience."

He added: Or have you never been?

Rumrill said: If I speak to you, then, as I am fairly certain is currently the case—unless this is only a rehearsal, which for the purposes of my statement amounts to the same thing—I have to give up thought. I am a mouth unsponsored, backed by no mind.

He added: Which is why I've prepared these notes.

Rumrill said: The greatest record I've set for silence—without speech addressed to someone else *who might understand it*—is three months. Though it's possible I have long since surpassed this landmark unawares.

He added: In recent years.

Rumrill said: By "in recent years," I mean the present, we'll say final period of my life, which years I might refer to, not coincidentally, as being themselves "mute," given that I no longer maintain any almanacs of my deeds or accomplishments, an activity in which I once took what I suspect was great satisfaction; for example, records as to the number of miles I might have walked on a given day, the number of words I might have read, the number of weeks I'd kept silent, deliberately or otherwise. Without an amanuensis or two to update my forsaken files, dormant in their cabinets beneath a gray loam of cat fur and my own innocent skin cells, it might seem to the eyes of a stranger that my life was a scholarly discipline whose sole devotee had at last lost interest and wandered off.

He added: His research consigned to oblivion.

Rumrill said: I imagine, however, that to the eyes of this stranger, if circumstances forced him or her, as you yourselves have been forced, to stand in my foyer confronted by myself and thus by a mass of apparently unassailable evidence that Rumrill does still walk the earth, however slowly, and however unambitious his orbit, this observer might note that while a student of Rumrilliana could no longer say with certainty whether I have or have not of late broken my own record of months without lucid speech, I have without a doubt now gone a record number of years without records, with no item added to the documentation that now occupies a number of filing cabinets on the first floor of my home, in what I am pleased to call my study. I recognize, of course, that this record number of years unrecorded has significance only in the context of a Rumrill, or the investigation of same, since the people in the big world beyond my walls—those people who are *not* Rumrill, I mean; for example, your own fine selves—spend their entire lives with no more sense of what they have or have not seen, said, tasted, or intended as my twenty cats have, severally or in aggregate, of the plots, characters, and sensations I might have retained from my dreams and then recounted to their forty torn and probably parasite-filled ears in moments of may I say reverie.

He added: And I may.

Rumrill said: It isn't that I challenged myself, in my almaniacal days, to maintain longer and longer periods of silence—any more than, now, record-less, I have challenged myself to break my record of "Longest Span Unrecorded." It's only that these periods began, with time, and given the circumstances of my life—after reaching their peak in the busy years that followed my resignation from my unimportant position at our town library—to accrue.

He added: And clot.

Rumrill said: I was raised, you see, to be a polite man named Rumrill, and I have been known to say hello to people, even strangers, should I be so unfortunate as to encounter them en route down one of my sovereign thoroughfares: on my way to the train station, for example, to ride to work, when I had work to which I needed to ride; on the way to the post office, for example, if I couldn't avoid such a trip, when the rates went up, which necessitated the purchase of new stamps; or perhaps to buy milk, or sugar, then so plentiful, which journeys became necessary after our grocer in her wisdom declined to continue her delivery service to my house, for reasons she did not see fit to share with kindly Mr. Rumrill, who tipped her boys so well and smelled by no means worse than the rest of our town, famed for its lack of functional gutters.

He added: I mean, for its rustic authenticity.

Rumrill said: Nonetheless, once I had retired into private life, shall we say, with fewer and fewer reasons to leave my house, and, concomitantly, more and more reasons to stay put, I soon winnowed down my exoduses to an ascetic minimum, and then further still. There are very few reasons, now, for me to go out at all.

He added: That superfluous, wasteful "out."

Rumrill said: This might seem a severe position for me to have adopted, but then I happen to know that your own home is so unpleasant an environment that you *invite* opportunities to take a turn in the open light, if only for a change of air. Whereas my habitat is adapted so perfectly to myself and myself to my habitat that such airings as are generally presumed to be beneficial to one's health are to me nothing more than ostentatious displays.

He added: Extravagance, by definition.

Rumrill said: I happen to know that you're awfully cramped in that apartment of yours, itself cramped in that cramped block of flats put up especially for your use, or rather for the use of yourselves as well as the other men and women of your generation, newly arrived in our town, blessed with low aspirations and a congenital tolerance for great altitudes. I remember when those buildings went up; I remember sturdy boys with acetylene torches in summer, high but not very on the red metal girders that would in time constrain you.

He added: And all your goods and chattel.

Rumrill said: I remember that they were underdressed in the heat, and that their faces were greenly visored to the sparks their torches spat. Despite the visors, I knew they could see our town beneath them; I knew that their eyes took in the older, smaller constructions below, which a local ordinance had kept squat and single-storied till then.

He added: Took them in, I mean, with contempt.

Rumrill said: There were girls too in those days, in shorts, on girl-bicycles ridden around the barricades, smug, where the traffic couldn't go—girls who came to us through some form of spontaneous generation, risen from the workers' torches' sparks where these touched our porous, inexpertly laid sidewalks, I assumed, since I'd never seen them before, and haven't since. I remember I found it impossible to imagine that such girls on such bicycles could have had origins or destinations; I found it impossible to imagine that they had feet or cunts beneath their respective coverings, that they had hair under their helmets; they circled and circled, the same ones or others who were no different.

He added: Reverie continued:

Rumrill: When I walked, in those days, as was in those days necessary, to and from the station where I waited to board the electric train to and from my shift at our town library, which operated at that time in our town's center, and at which institution I was to work for more years than you have been able to own property or drink liquor in any of our neighborhood bars, I favored a particular route, unsurprisingly, and found unsurprisingly that your new buildings would force me to abandon my preferred route through our neighborhood. Though of course by "your buildings" I mean not your buildings as such but the accumulation of similar if not identical red girders and coffee-stained bicuspids of concrete sunk in the weeds and splinters of our barren lots, where at one time enough leftover notions and knickknacks from long-extinct shops and carts had been abandoned in the dirt that the vicious children of our older, more established town families would go there to stuff their pockets mornings and evenings, in search of whatever undamaged trinkets might still be saleable: water-filled demi-globes in which mock coal dust rather than mock snow drifted in no tide to settle on a miniature sculpture of our town hall; outsize earrings with train-car pendants; dolls' boots; once-unspoiled coins of whatever denomination mutilated by penny-fed machines (since chopped into firewood) to bear the embossed image of our town's single bridge.

He added: Saleable, I mean, to rubes and newcomers.

Rumrill said: That is to say, the construction of your new residences, built to accommodate the influx of young men and women to this town—a town that was then, by contrast, relatively prosperous and mildew-free—interrupted my preferred route, to which I had grown accustomed, perhaps sentimentally attached, and littered this once safe corridor with roadblocks and the chirrups of detouring bicycles and let us not forget the vapid eyeballs of men and women unaccustomed to the sight of Rumrill. Too, they would in time—when tarted up with walls and roofs and telephone cables—interrupt the theretofore-unimpeded view from my bedroom window of our cowering township beneath what my neighbors were pleased to call its sky.

He added: Uninfected by aircraft.

Rumrill said: My neighbors were in those days heard to say from their patios and from inside the gazebos that regularly polyped in white out of their as-yet emerald lawns—or, if on the move, in conversation with their spouses or coworkers from beneath floppy hats as elegant shoes crunched through the autumn canopy of brittle brown worm parasols recently fallen from our trees—that your buildings, when complete, would be *eyesores* in or to our community. As they said this, and then as they repeated it to be better heard over the leaf-crackle raised by their confident feet or the *Schrammelmusik* trio perched behind them on one of the spotless white benches so well tended in my youth by our town's sanitation department, hard though this may be for you to believe, they could not have been aware—save in the most atavistic crenellations of their neighborly brains—what this barbarous disyllable would communicate to Rumrill's ear: namely, that the pain of their disinheritance was akin to the niggling pink eruptions that frequently boiled out of the sebaceous glands of their stye-prone brats.

He added: Warm water sometimes helps.

Rumrill said: It takes no great effort to imagine their words overheard by my younger self, secreted on an adjacent balcony—forced as I was in those days to live in a thickset brick apartment house like their own. As I listened to their complaints, I felt in quantities I cannot accurately measure dollops in unequal parts of sympathy, satisfaction, and confusion.

He added: Or so my records indicate.

Rumrill said: When I overheard my then-neighbors complain about the ugliness and inconvenience of your buildings, whose advent I recall was announced daily by early-morning jackhammer blats, I found their comments—addressed, fancifully, to the secret chiefs who had made the decision to build your high-rise tenements and build them to be such provocative sores—difficult to comprehend. It was evident to me, with my aseptic eyes cocked at our violated horizon, that these new buildings, your damp and narrow warrens, had been designed by men and women out in the big world who had been made ignorant by circumstance (or force of will) of the likelihood that their work would ever be evaluated as objects worthy of aesthetic consideration.

He added: Any more than a ferret could be considered an adding machine.

Rumrill said: Inasmuch as any considerations beyond the efficient use of space—how best to cram in as many of your bovine coevals as possible—were in the minds of those men and women responsible for hiring in turn those sturdy girder-men to build your buildings out of materials no less sturdy, I imagine their foremost concern would have been that men and women like yourselves be able to *understand* how best to employ the kind of *Lebensraum* with which they had provided you. They would want you to learn, for instance, how to make efficient use of not very much space, physical space as well as what my once-neighbors might have called social space, since you must I'm sure be able to smell each other's shit day and night, and therefore set aside for the duration of your stay, thanks to necessity or effort of will, such categories as "pretty" or "ugly."

He added: And so respect the nature of your new environment.

Rumrill said: Your buildings, then, might be considered pedagogical tools, intended not for the natives of our town—all of us past rescue—but for the next generation, young men and women like yourselves who would be sent to us as proof positive of the town planners' argument that their buildings were needful additions to our putatively eyesoreless town, for where else could we put you? Likewise, your lives in their apartments would, *pace* my once-neighbors, demonstrate that even such unlovely spaces might indeed be lived in comfortably.

He added: QED.

Rumrill said: Such buildings serve to teach you the benefits, if any, of a life lived in your buildings. Such buildings teach you *how* to live in your buildings.

He added: And you've learned.

Rumrill said: When you eat dinner in your narrowness and damp, you eat in the way your buildings have taught you to eat; when you crawl over each other and navigate your hopelessly knotted sheets to fuck in the night—or, who knows, on a weekend morning—you crawl and fuck in the manners your buildings have dictated. You eat or fuck or think of that cherubic young man with the dictionary of Old English who smiled at you across the aisle on the train one morning, all in the manner your buildings have taught you to eat or fuck or think.

He added: Neither pretty nor ugly.

Rumrill said: If my neighbors of those days had complained instead that the intrusion of your buildings represented a differently conceived organization of space and therefore behavior, indeed one that felt inimical to that with which they'd become accustomed—taught to them in youth by our neighborhood and its houses, bricks, and balconies (till then designed exclusively by men and women long dead, advocates of no social program, who had, in life, in work, in all likelihood, been precisely the sort of men and women who would have evaluated their handiwork in such terms as "pretty" or "ugly")—I would have understood what was meant when they called the new high-rises *eyesores*. If my once-neighbors had said that the addition of buildings such as yours to our town had even before their completion altered our common environment in ways that we could not yet discern or articulate, and that these changes already felt to them inconvenient, perhaps sinister, even "ugly"—I assure you I would have nodded my head and given a friendly smile.

He added: A gesture familiar in my day as indicative of assent.

Rumrill said: When we townspeople ate or fucked, or walked as was our right to and from the train station by whatever route we found most agreeable, or perambulated really to any point on the compass, contingent of course upon how the changed layout of our town might revise those preferences— for even our preferences have been taught to us—we no longer in those days set about these things in our neighborhood as we remembered it, but in a new world entirely, our neighborhood-plus-your-buildings: a foreign place that might as well, despite its apparent familiarity, have been Istanbul. Even in our complaints—the formulation of which I believe gave my then-neighbors perhaps the principal pleasure in lives by no means empty of such self-indulgence—we were obliged to complain with present-day thoughts couched in our words of Anglo-Saxon or less sturdy descents by way of the preferred routes or least-resented detours our neighborhood-plus-your-buildings dictated we complain.

He added: Routes followed without our knowledge or consent.

Rumrill said: I mean that since the men and women who designed your buildings had only one theoretical concern, which was that their work serve to welcome the greatest possible number of new transplants to our town in the least possible square footage (albeit a significant amount of airspace), and since too their corridors and stairwells even in those early days gave people an altogether ominous impression, not unlike that of a newly cleaned abattoir—or indeed *unlike* one only in that your buildings are not often cleaned—it follows that part of what you've learned from your apartment is to find excuses to be away from it. I am happy for your sakes that, whether or not you are hired, you will have today the opportunity to learn from *my* home that your lives to date have been circumscribed and unlovely.

He added: You're welcome.

Rumrill said: It follows too that part of what I've learned from my own home is that I've learned more than enough of what the big world outside its walls might have to teach me. I leave the mysteries of the big world to those unfortunates whose homes and minds that world has so profaned as to strand them without a refuge between their walls or neuro- and viscerocrania in which to shelter from its rains and knives.

He added: And wild dogs.

Rumrill said: I hope, given all this, you'll understand

why I will ask that while you are resident in my home, should you be found suitable—the decision is out of my hands, really, even while it is mine to make—you not alter, add, adapt, or subtract pieces of furniture, or such decorations as there are, or any structures be they large or small—from the silt-cushioned seeds stuck between the slats of my kitchen's wooden floor, to the orderly disposition of the forks and knives and spoons and olive spears a few steps distant—from or in or to this house. This is no more than I ask of myself.

He added: That is, of Rumrill.

Rumrill said: I gave up alterations, adaptations, additions an indeterminate number of years ago; I no more alter the various elements of my own home than I would those in a stranger's apartment had I forced entrance into it in quest of his or her intimate correspondence. I haven't painted or even cleaned certain portions of my own house for many years—for many years, I mean, since whatever point during my almanac days I decided to minimize as much as possible any changes in the more or less stable system that is my and my cats' daily routine: the same three windows opened, the same side of the bed slept on, the same routes taken between rooms.

He added: And the same words used to describe this.

Rumrill said: You will understand, then, why I will ask you, if you are invited farther into my home—this vestibule, let us say, is an intermediate step: the embassy, the airlock—not to move any of the objects you find there so much as a centimeter from their appointed places. You will understand, then, why I will ask you to restore any items that you might accidentally or despite my entreaties and with some inexplicable hubris in your hearts remove or shift or nudge with hip or shoulder from their appointed places back to whatever positions in your dim and constrained perceptions appears close to if not indistinguishable from the locations in which you first found them.

He added: Presumably appointed.

Rumrill said: I used to keep a snow globe at my desk when as a younger man I worked at our public library. Whenever I arrived at work in the morning, or came back from my regular lunchtime assignation in the section of the old Dewey decimal stacks devoted to Byzantine architecture, I would readjust this snow globe with a show of great irritation: videlicet, any number of exasperated sighs and curses at near-conversational volume and an inventory of scowls at whomever happened to be near my portion of the counter while I made said snow-globe adjustments.

He added: To ward off unauthorized interference.

Rumrill said: I wanted to give my coworkers the impression that I was the sort of person who never failed to notice when his belongings had been moved so much as a centimeter from their appointed places. "The impression," because I am *not* in fact the sort of person who never fails to notice when his belongings have been moved so much as a centimeter from their appointed places.

He added: Not in centimeters, anyhow.

Rumrill said: My particular genius, as I am pleased to call it, is for the inverse procedure. That is, while I may not have a memory so precise as to be able to discern when my most dear and secret possessions have been moved a centimeter from their appointed places—or indeed to remember your names, or in what order occurred the catastrophes that have brought we three together for our delightful discussion on this cloudless or cloudy day—I am more than satisfactorily skilled when it comes to interference with *other people*'s things.

He added: And have never been caught.

Rumrill said: If I'd rifled through your most dear and secret things, in your narrow and damp apartment, my face and hands cut into noxious rhombuses by the glossy orange pattern on your wallpaper, I can assure you that you would never suspect that the clear light of Rumrill had ever been shed in your home. Whatever unease you might feel on taking a peek in order to reassure yourself that those dear and secret things were still intact in their appointed places, you would mistake for nothing more than your own distaste for the duplicity demonstrated toward your spouse when first you lied to keep them (I mean, those objects) safe.

He added: "Why, *what* dear and secret things, *Liebling*?"

Rumrill said: It follows that my discomfort with the conversation of my fellow *Homo sapiens* isn't the only reason I'm unhappy to have welcomed, or at least allowed, you into my vestibule. Even now, stranded by politeness and my not inconsiderable bulk in this dirty and confining antechamber, decorated by the wind that once would elbow past me as I came or went on this or that errand, and which has deposited here in aid of who knows what program these bleak and desiccated leaves, these mummified flies and mummified fly aspirations, you have made changes, aural-olfactory-visual-chemical, to an environment and so set of procedures and so mode of thought I have strived to preserve in as near an invariable state as the big world's little munificence toward order will allow.

He added: Unmaliciously, for your parts, I do not doubt.

Rumrill said: Nor can I doubt that you're a lovely young couple, in spite of your monstrousness in my eyes. I mean that I imagine there are standards according to which you would be deemed nothing less than a lovely young couple, *such* a lovely young couple, without peer in our town, well known to be so poor or rich in lovely young couples.

He added: Though mister smells of pickles and missus is a little popeyed.

Rumrill said: While here am I, all my wits mustered to welcome you, to listen to your silly names as you introduce yourselves into my home, intrude upon its atmosphere with your unlikely bodies and sounds. Here am I to take stock of the infelicitous manner providence saw fit to put your arms and legs and eyes into their respective sockets, and then your clothing thereupon in its infelicitous droop and unfortunate oilslick of color, not to mention the identical wilted asterisks of hair under your wetly crumpled hats.

He added: All present and correct.

Rumrill said: Provided, I mean, that I am not

still alone with my cats in what I am pleased to call my study; that I am not after all at my typewriter with these pages after all intended only for use in the unlikely event anyone comes at last to be interviewed in my vestibule. Because, after all, what sort of desperate character would be tempted to answer my ad?

He added: Provided I remembered to post it.

Rumrill said: Not that I'm sorry you made me wait, that you took such a time to make up your minds to inquire about the so-called positions you hope to fill in my household. This reprieve gave me a pleasant few weeks to decide upon which foot from the two available I ought to lean my plausible weight when finally beginning my exordium; to decide with which side of my face I ought to favor you as I take in your poor imitation of adult attire; time to compose my thoughts.

He added: My arias, my instructions, my denials.

Rumrill said: And, as you will see from this sheaf of papers, thick as a book, which I've brought from my study to serve as an *aide-mémoire*, or should I say *Gedächtnisstütze*, in our conversation, I have a great deal to say to you. Or else, it is safe to assume, if not to you in particular, that I have a great deal to *say*, as they say, *period*.

He added: Or *full stop*, if that's your poison.

Rumrill said: The machine on which I typed my notes was inherited from a man who did not intend that I keep it. I typed my notes using the remainder of a store of paper I bought as a younger man to devote to a secretarial job that was, evidently, left incomplete, given the surplus of materials I retain in my several filing cabinets.

He added: Which are no more mine, really, than the typewriter.

Rumrill said: I am meant now, my notes tell me, to thank you again for your interest in the positions of cat-sitter and caretaker in my home, which interest bespeaks either great despondency or great generosity on your parts, it's hard to say. It's also hard to say in what way I might have promised to remunerate whomever is awarded the position.

He added: What could I have that you would want?

Rumrill said: I say "thank you *again*," but I can't remember whether I've already had cause to thank you for anything. I know you've done nothing much thus far to *oblige* me to thank you, but "thank you" is often said for reasons other than gratitude, just as "again" is often employed strictly for reasons of rhythm.

He added: Meter more than sense.

Rumrill said: What you have to understand is that to fiddle with any of my belongings, be they dear or secret or otherwise, no matter how inconveniently you may find them placed, would be to fiddle with my understanding of my environment, and by extension my ability, retroactively, to know precisely which belongings must not be moved so that my environment and understanding and so personality remain recognizable to me. Never mind that it might seem a small thing to you to push my overstuffed armchair, scored by innumerable cat-scratches, from the northeast to the northwest corners of what I am pleased to call my sitting room.

He added: Or:

Rumrill said: Never mind that it might seem a small thing for you to push my armchair to a place nearer a window, perhaps the one in my study. Never mind that it might seem entirely natural, indeed trifling, to scrape my floors and scuff my carpeting so that you could read, Missus Pickles, a glossy magazine there, in comfort, in the natural light, where the colors in the photographs in said magazine would seem particularly vivid, and as such serve I'm sure as a better distraction from what must be a life of continual puzzlement and anxiety.

He added: Complaints we would dignify overmuch if we were to label them "discontent."

Rumrill said: But such interventions are *not* a small thing, *Mutter und Vater* Pickles, since Rumrill-with-his-chair-in-the-northwest-corner or Rumrill-with-his-chair-God-only-knows-where, is, to me, a stranger: alien to Rumrill prime, this Rumrill, Rumrill-with-his-chair-in-its-proper-place. Indeed, such a Rumrill would be too alien for myself to anticipate what unusual measures this probably deranged personage might undertake to revenge the wanton murder of his predecessor.

He added: Himself a bit bizarre.

Rumrill said: Already, with yourselves in my home, here by the front door, in my vestibule or foyer, I find I am not the Rumrill I was before the moment I opened said door so that you could step inside out of what seems as ever the inclement weather beyond. Which is perhaps why I still haven't reconciled myself to this peripeteia, why I haven't, as they say, "asked you in"; though here too must be an *in*, certainly you've come *into* my house, vestibule or no: I can see the snow melt or the rain evaporate from the shoes or boots I have instructed you to remove.

He added: I have become, for one thing, quite garrulous!

Rumrill said: Apropos, may I say that through my open door as you stepped in I saw little clouds frisk across the morning or evening sky? Which clouds looked by no means significant enough to be responsible, down here below the tropopause, at the height of the three stone stairs that access Rumrill's house—squat in the fashion of most detached residences in our town—for having left you both so wet and weary from your walk?

He added: Little round lucid clouds.

Rumrill said: To provide some historical context for what I'm sure you consider an irritating foible on the part of your prospective employer, I can tell you that it was initially decided that my household would tolerate no amendments to its geography not for my own sake but for the convenience of my twenty cats, who become confused whenever circumstances distress their familiar landscape. In my younger days I would, like yourselves, throw away a piece of furniture without a moment's anxiety—for instance, a sofa, its soft tissue worn down to the point of inhospitality—and so permit the intrusion of sturdy men into my home to remove it by way of the front door (which was, to all appearances, too small to permit such egress), and again, subsequently, to effect the delivery of its replacement.

He added: (Likewise impossible.)

Rumrill said: My cats' reaction could be described as analogous to that of my old neighbors had they looked outside the windows of their tree-shaded homes one morning and seen not a block of ugly new tenements on the horizon but a different horizon entirely. Twin suns sink behind a lake, as strange moons circle, and black stars rise.

He added: And so forth.

Rumrill said: On the subject of sofas, the previous owners of *this* house left a green one behind after the flooding that reduced the property's price to what we might call the purview of Rumrill. The most notable feature of this sofa, aside from the frond-shaped stains where the water level lapped it, was its boniness.

He added: *Le canapé sans chair* (The Fleshless Settee), a tragedy in one act by M. Rumrill.

Rumrill said: It was bony, said *canapé*, even before my cats and myself wore away what flesh we found on it. Its continued erosion beneath my big and their little bodies, in succession or parallel, on the days and nights of its tenure in my home, reduced its thin, cheap cushions to nearly nothing in short order.

He added: Upholstery a dead art in our town even then.

Rumrill said: Yet I found the green sofa to be more and not less comfortable as it went scraggier still. This in much the way I once preferred to rest my head on the sharp upraised knees and not breasts of a librarian you are unlikely to have met.

He added: Or ex-librarian.

Rumrill said: Indeed, the ossification of the green sofa was accelerated by my penchant for its favors over the more corpulent option provided by my bed, on the second floor, or the first floor above the ground floor, if that's your poison. I almost wished, then, that I knew people who might come over to visit my house, the better to displace me, at night, from my regular sleeping place.

He added: Which I would be so polite as to vacate in their favor.

Rumrill said: Downstairs, I would pass the night splayed in an attitude of apparent discomfort, if not agony, my head resting on no cushion but a smooth wooden armrest the circumference and density of a pipe or bottle of beer. I would be attended in time by ballast in the form of those cats courageous enough to perch on me not in the relative safety of my wide, flat, soft bed, but here, in attitudes of acute instability, on my knees or shoulders, askew.

He added: Boulders on buttes.

Rumrill said: Initially, I repeat, I imposed the aforementioned constraints on my environment for the convenience of my cats, not for myself—if any state of affairs may be described as convenient for or to them. Suffice it to say that my cats appear to undergo a traumatic change, and thereby adopt new habits, places of repose, routes between rooms, and food preferences when the disposition of their environment is altered.

He added: A disruption to the more or less self-sustained system comprised by my household, which, in its continued function, constitutes what we might call the stable axle of our life, from which I depart when I go out into the big world and return when I have concluded my business with same.

Rumrill said: Certainly, in time, after some or another change had been made, I would console myself that it appeared my cats had "gotten used" to whatever was now different in my home, that they no longer seemed perturbed by it, and had found ways to reassert their old personalities and habits. But this was a false conclusion, not to say a false comfort, for how could this apparent restoration of normalcy be in fact an acclimatization to the new conditions that obtained in our environment when my notion of normalcy with regard to my cats was defined for myself by no other means than this same observation of their behavior, habits, places of repose, routes between rooms, food preferences, and so forth, all within the till-recently invariable context of this same till-recently invariable environment?

He added: Now very slightly varied.

Rumrill said: It would be more accurate to say that the cats who had "gotten used" to whatever new arrangement of my belongings were no longer then the same animals. It would be more accurate to say the cats who had lived under the old order had been washed away; that a catastrophe had made the tides rise until the chill waters had claimed those poor creatures who had prospered throughout the reign, for example, of our much-mourned green sofa.

He added: Which eventually gave me an awful splinter and so could no longer rely on my protection.

Rumrill said: They were no more the same

animals now than my neighbors were the same neighbors with whom I had been forced to contend before your eyesores were constructed, aside from the seeming continuity of their appearances: two legs and two eyes, floppy hats, and all the other impedimenta. They were no more the same animals now than I was the same Rumrill, confronted with different neighbors and a different neighborhood and so household and town.

He added: Washed by the floodtide.

Rumrill said: My home is only my home, and my cats only my cats, and my Rumrill only my Rumrill—inasmuch as these are mine—because those unavoidable and insidious mutations that have till this day been visited within the little world of my home upon our sovereign thoroughfares have left our shapes still largely recognizable to the unstable locus of perception that is this Rumrill here before you, still and I think very considerately ministering to your as-yet-unvoiced queries and concerns. I ask you to retain your questions till the end of our interview, but I do so with the knowledge that the Mister and Missus Pickles who shall greet me when my remarks have been concluded will no longer care to hear whatever answer the absence of which now makes you so itchy.

He added: But whose absence will in time be a comfort.

Rumrill said: It is imperative, moreover, to the Rumrill who prepared this series of notes, that not only three-dimensional objects such as sofas or catheters be left in their appointed places, but that this same respect be shown as well to what might be termed chronological objects: whichever activities along the timeline of a Rumrill's day must be maintained—that is, performed—only at such and such an hour and minute, and must be left in their appointed places, however dusty or in need of a polish with some caustic cleanser and a *schmatte* up there on what I might term the temporal mantelpiece. (If you will allow me this flight of fancy.)

He added: (Or whatever sort of flight it may be.)

Rumrill said: I could cite as example the evacuation of my bowels, which takes place promptly at nine A.M., except in case of emergency, in which eventuality make-up sessions may be profitably scheduled at eleven A.M., two thirty P.M., or six P.M. You do not need to memorize this particular schedule as I will be only too pleased to provide you an illustrated itinerary after our conversation.

He added: With carbon copies on pink onionskin.

Rumrill said: Don't think that what is ostensibly a private act has no effect upon my household and its twenty tenants. I do not forbid my cats entry to the bathroom when I am engaged with my toilette.

He added: How they weep when thus forbade.

Rumrill said: It is impossible in any case to forbid my cats entry to any room, thanks to their greater understanding of this building architecturally and may I say phenomenally. My cats are everywhere in my home; they are coterminous with my home, or vice versa.

He added: Which makes it all the more curious that none have joined us here in the foyer.

Rumrill said: In all honesty, I discovered years ago during an interval when my cats' interest in the process of my toilette had dwindled to the point wherein they might a few days a week prefer to focus their attentions at nine, eleven, two thirty, or six upon the picture window in my study—which looks upon a sidewalk that was not then so impervious to the blemish of an accidental passerby as it is in the here and now—that this disruption of our habitual perambulations and acts respectively of witness and being oneself borne witness to in fact *impeded* my internal coordination to the point that the evacuation of my bowels proved impossible. I was forced to corral a number of my cats and set them in privileged positions inside my bathroom, boulders on buttes, so as to afford them the best view of my activities and provide me in turn with the greatest assurance of being seen by their eyes in the blinkless collaboration my bowels found so needful.

He added: And by extension, my thoughts; and by extension, my sensations.

Rumrill said: One is reminded of the widely recorded phenomenon of a pathological inability to evacuate one's bowels save while reading some form of literature fetched into one's bathroom for this very purpose. One is reminded, by extension, of the Talmudic ban on the enjoyment of secular literature in any site whatever save one's place of evacuation.

He added: Number of references to cats in the Talmud—unknown.

Rumrill said: To complicate matters, insofar as the recordless period of my life now underway, whenever I do leave my home and its twenty cats to run an errand, I find that whatever evidence might persist in easy reach to confirm that I have in fact gone out is quickly subsumed into the silt of this sameness on my return: perhaps, I think, I was mistaken when I noted that my stores of rice had been depleted, that I'd long since had the gas disconnected in a fit of pique, or else paid this month's bill in advance in a moment of misplaced enthusiasm? Evidence is broken down, digested, assimilated, made congruent with the surface of my daily life, which because it advances by such erasures has the consistency of a dream.

He added: Albeit one in which I am allowed to retain my trousers.

Rumrill said: I know from my meticulous and may I say lifelong scrutiny of the strange though by no means unique case of Mr. Rumrill that, on his return, which is to say my own, from my upcoming journey, I will almost certainly accuse you of all manner of malfeasance with regard to the aforementioned prohibitions, no matter what pains you've taken to follow my instructions. I mean, for example, the molestation of those objects that are most dear to me, and secret.

He added: Whatever, and wherever, they may be.

Rumrill said: Do your best to bear up under my denunciations and refrain from any futile displays of self-righteousness or even the exercise of your natural senses of dignity, if that's the word; perhaps you might even consider my inevitable suspicion and ingratitude to be a portion of your rightful remuneration, if you are hired: if you are to be servants in my peculiar country—if not so distant as the Levant—you are of necessity obliged to accept payment in the local currency. Do not, moreover, let the certainty of your eventual condemnation lead you to believe that I harbor doubts as to your strength of character: you seem to me a trustworthy young couple, or at least not notably untrustworthy, if we take into account the circumstances and era and environment into which you were born, and which conditions your birth so singularly failed to improve.

He added: *Brine and Punishment: A Social, Economic, and Cultural History of the Pickle Dynasty*, by A. N. Rumrill.

Rumrill said: I will not ask you to do or not do anything while in my employ that I was not myself expected to do or not do when I, almost as young as you are now, first made my debut into the tortuous discipline of cat care. Let me confess that I myself once pet-sat a house with *thirty* cats.

He added: Or, rather, pet-sat the cats.

Rumrill said: That house is empty now, wherever I left it. Or else, there's simply nobody of interest living there.

He added: If it has not, for instance, burned down in the meantime.

Rumrill said: I mention this to put our own predicament, which is to say yours, into perspective. To sit only twenty cats, by comparison, ought to be simplicity itself.

He added: Simpler by ten cats, in fact.

Rumrill said: You might say that those absent ten are of all my cats the most important, the most in need of care. Care, I mean, to ensure that they are never acquired.

He added: Those absent ten the buffer between myself and what you'd have to call eccentricity.

Rumrill said: When I accepted the position of cat-sitter, which decision had profound consequences for my life to come, not to mention my CV, the owner of those thirty cats, an Austrian—whose name, of unknown provenance, was Brocklebank, and whose profession before retirement was watch repair—left me a series of typed instructions, as thick as a book. He had already for a good many years been one of those people for whom a nest of cats is a substitute for engagement with the world.

He added: The big world, that is, beyond his walls.

Rumrill said: You might argue that, however eccentric its occupant, the inside of a house is still a part of the big world, with all the qualities thereof; for example the quality of a space from which and into which one can travel, and inside of which one has the privilege of perambulation say upstairs and down, and really to any point on the compass. As I am not at this stage prepared to argue the point, let us say instead that Mr. Brocklebank had become one of those people for whom having cats is a substitute for engagement with one's own *species*.

He added: Or indeed one's own Brocklebank.

Rumrill said: How does one name thirty cats? How does one name even twenty?

He added: Ask Brocklebank, if you can find him.

Brocklebank writes: Naming is a function of time.

Rumrill said: He was already an educated man when he came to this country. I don't know what he'd intended to become instead of a repairer of watches, but he was prevented, or unable, to live that life, that imagined life whose loss I'm sure was a source of no small distress for him.

He added: Watch repair a desperate improvisation.

Rumrill said: It takes no great effort for me to imagine Mr. and Mrs. Brocklebank in Vienna, anxious but sleepy in the rustle of prewar springtime leaves. Mr. and Mrs. Brocklebank on their green sofa exhorted by friends and relatives to leave town and country while such was still possible.

He added: If such was still possible.

Rumrill said: How they yawned, however, and snuffled, and stretched their calves, which ached from so many healthful constitutionals around the Türkenschanzpark. "Oh, but it's such a nice day— we'll flee tomorrow, we'll be afraid tomorrow, don't be such a sourpuss."

He added: And then, to one another, "A *bissel* coffee, my dear?"

Rumrill said: In fact, Brocklebank escaped to some temperate and brightly colored pre-revolutionary nation without much difficulty. Mrs. Brocklebank, on the other hand, stayed behind to await word that it was safe for her to proceed.

He added: And was therefore apprehended.

Brocklebank writes: Having come to believe that naming is also about the *suspension* of time.

Rumrill said: I confess that I have little other information to offer concerning Mrs. Brocklebank. Besides, I mean, the circumstances of her demise many years later.

He added: In our dear little town.

Rumrill said: In sum, I can report that the numbers on her arm were 17711, and that she could not have children. She set her clock daily for 7:23 A.M. but routinely remained in bed a half-hour more.

He added: Use made of the popular "snooze" button.

Rumrill said: She menstruated rarely, at irregular intervals, until menopause, at which time, before it ceased entirely, she menstruated regularly and too often. The lines on her face were present even when she was young, but she only became self-conscious about them when she reached middle age, despite their manifest continuity.

He added: Which probably made her easy to draw.

Brocklebank writes: Existing as we do only by the clear, persistent image of ourselves.

Rumrill said: How I came to know Brocklebank is easier to report. Late in life, alone, a retiree in our small town, after the purportedly natural death of his sterile wife, and after the acquisition of his many housecats, the old man, still in possession of most if not all of what I am pleased to call his "marbles," became quite a reader.

He added: Tasteless and profligate.

Rumrill said: He came to the public library twice a week, and this was where I made his acquaintance:

I a member of the staff and he a patron with colossal croissant ears, an alpine landslide of a face—still a patriot, despite all. He hobbled in from the underground train station, then hobbled out again with a new brace of books, always in the same plastic bag from the same chain store printed with the same German name.

He added: And filled with the worst trash imaginable.

Rumrill said: As a retired childless widower in a town and where he'd intended to maintain a wife for company, Brocklebank had plenty of time on his hands. I am not unaware that an old watch repairman with time on his hands is an invitation to perpetrate a play on words.

He added: Which invitation will be declined.

Rumrill said: Was the acquisition of his great many housecats a project that Brocklebank had already formulated before his arrival in our town, and which was only made possible by the death of his sterile wife? Or would their acquisition and the subsequent composition of his opus on the subject of their care have proceeded even had his sterile wife survived her illness?

He added: "Opus" and "illness," so to call them.

Rumrill said: In time I took upon myself the responsibility for Brocklebank's pets on those occasions he left our town on one of his mysterious junkets. I assumed this responsibility without coercion in exchange for a little extra pocket money, not to mention open access to the Brocklebankian larder, my salary at the library insufficient for the needs, not to say appetite, of a healthy young Rumrill if unsupplemented by the income afforded by the occasional odd job (or else the sale of some petty but nonetheless excruciatingly mourned piece of personal, or, in time, stolen property; or the clumsy *Erpressung* by anonymous letter (penned with the less favored of my two hands on thin, blue airmail paper) of those neighbors still naive or brazen enough to discuss private matters on their balconies within range of my exquisite hearing). To Brocklebank's mind, he and Young Rumrill had in the weeks and months grown if not "close" than certainly "chummy" over the stamps and cardstock of the library's circulation desk, which I was obliged to man on regular occasions.

He added: As a sort of penance.

Rumrill said: When my colleagues were unavailable, perhaps away at lunch or else in the process of who knows what depravity through the plausible fibers of their semi-formal attire in some ill-frequented section of the stacks—or just united in what they mistook for a jolly chuckle, from some concealed location, at my own apparently improbable apparel, behind my back though very much within range of said exquisite hearing—Brocklebank would buttonhole me about his great project, of which I understood nothing then, my disinterested smiles and nods an unintended encouragement to him. Soon enough my time was split between library and *Schloss* Brocklebank, and I would—in hopes of a comradely rapprochement with my coworkers—bring stories back to the library about the old man's numerous idiosyncrasies—humorous digests of the life and thought of Mr. Brocklebank—so as to profit further from the old man's not inconsiderable store of strangeness.

He added: Glorious, because rare, moments of collusion with my peers.

Brocklebank writes: Yet believing I do not go out of my way to cultivate my personality, my independence.

Rumrill said: What hilarity the day Mr. Brocklebank came into the public library with a cheaply printed magazine, of which in those days many were still published. What hilarity as Brocklebank showed it to me, to us, limp and sodden (the magazine), with wheezing satisfaction (the man).

He added: Done a mischief (both) by the incessant rain.

Rumrill said: It transpired that some halfwit out in the big world had agreed to devote space in his or her moribund quarterly to a few pages of Brocklebank's notes, practical as well as metaphysical, on the subject of his cats, which the old man had sent in without cover letter. This was not a cat-care magazine, I hasten to add, if any such still existed, but a journal of sixty-eight or seventy-four pages minus advertisements, decorated on its paper wrap with a painted illustration in Troubadour Style of an enormous octopoidal creature with eleven envious eyes trained, I could not help but think, upward into our own big world of depth and time, rather than down at the victim suspended in its violet-fleshed tentacles, her face and figure not unlike those of the coworker with whom I snuck on occasion into the stacks; she (the victim) reclined provocatively albeit with secondary sexual characteristics hidden by inconvenient orange strips of her torn and limp hazard suit, her own eyes aimed not on we readers but at the words that floated above her captor, in an extra wide serif: *Tremendous Science-Fiction Tales*.

He added: Unless I mean *Thrilling* or *Astonishing*.

Rumrill said: Encouraged by this one and only success, as he was pleased to call it, as a cat-care theoretician, and insensible of how he had been made ridiculous, it wasn't long before Brocklebank thought he should hire someone not only to take care of his cats in his absence—for he intended to continue his travels to more temperate climes, and then there would be invitations to go on lecture tours soon enough—but in his presence to sit at his desk adjacent to his many filing cabinets and produce neat typescripts of his work, from holograph or dictation. Brocklebank, you see, was arthritic, more and more so—which phrase implies the passage of time—and was given in any case to tremors; soon he wouldn't be able to hold a pen, he wouldn't be able to work the shift key, he wouldn't be able to sit or stand, he wouldn't be able to read or not read, he wouldn't be able to stay asleep or awake, he would become untenable.

He added: With carbon copies on pink onionskin.

Rumrill said: I was gang-pressed, then, into service as Brocklebank's factotum; this in addition to my other duties, civic and feline. It wasn't long before the work I did for Brocklebank began to impinge upon my real work, that is, my library work, the work from which I earned the greater part of my livelihood.

He added: As I was pleased to call it.

Rumrill said: Now I often found myself late back to the library from a lunchtime errand for Brocklebank, thus deprived to my regret of another in the all-too-limited series of assignations it was fated that I would be able to enjoy with my supervisor, who disdained even to look at me in reproach when at last I returned. Would that I could pass a typed note to Young Rumrill from our unruly present day, a word of fraternal advice, to the effect that the memory of a pound of rice purchased or gas bill mailed on behalf of a screwy old man will be in no way a solace to us in our own years of decline.

He added: Expenses reimbursed biweekly.

Rumrill said: Well you might ask, since I was in no way obligated to carry out these tasks, nor indeed continue my acquaintance *ex post facto* with the old man, given my distaste for the verities of Brocklebankian existence—his crooked back, his humorless shuffle, his ontological instability, his mucilage-green suspenders—why I allowed my work for Brocklebank to supplant my work at the library, which was, as they say, steady. Did I find some greater enjoyment in my errands for Brocklebank; did they engage what I am pleased to call my attention to a greater degree than did my other responsibilities?

He added: All opinions welcome.

Brocklebank writes: Having become used, where one's own work is concerned, to clearing away all obstacles by means of immense intellectual effort and over so many years finding oneself constantly faced with new obstacles against which all thinking, all power of invention, all energy, all ideas, proved helpless, for a man for whom ideas have been every-thing, this means nothing less than the total collapse of things, unless he has come to find support, in ever increasing measure, in a belief in something higher, beyond.

Rumrill said: Brocklebank claimed to have been to many foreign countries, more than I would have considered proper, and he knew them all well enough to be able to advise me, whether or not I cared to listen, where—in the unlikely event I were to travel abroad—I could treat myself to an affordable but authentic and above all perfectly hygienic meal in any one of them. By way of the sort of simplistic inver-sion I often mistake for wit, I wondered how well, by contrast, he knew his own house, and adopted hometown.

He added: Those unsent letters of his wife's, for example, hidden behind the green radiator in the guest bedroom.

Brocklebank writes: For a long time wondering how to make for myself a space into which I could retreat, where I could find quiet, where I could see, hear, where I would be able to concentrate, where I would be isolated from the world around but still able to participate in it.

Rumrill said: While the old man was away, in the old days, I would arrive at his house after my work-day at the library and then some time alone aboard the electric train over our town's single bridge and through the intervening residential neighborhoods. I would still in those first hours after work be perfumed by the substances secreted by my supervisor, the librarian with whom I went regularly on our lunch breaks into the infrequently visited rear stacks of the library to engage in activities more or less novel to me at this time.

He added: And, come to think of it, novel since.

Rumrill said: I would open Brocklebank's door and replenish the food and water in the many bowls found in his cellar, on his ground floor, on the floor above his ground floor, and in his Austrian attic. Likewise, I would deplete, if that's the word, the amount of excrement in the correspondingly numerous litter boxes.

He added: For example in the guest bedroom with the aforementioned green radiator and the writing desk once the property of Mrs. Brocklebank, which I believe is properly called a "drop-front secretary."

Rumrill said: It did not occur to me, befuddled by the smell of cunt, which seemed to waft even from the handrails, even from the pantographs of our municipal railway, to count the cats I encountered as I perambulated on my rounds on my two legs between Brocklebank's rooms, empty of any unfeline odor. To count the cats did not occur to me because, back when he had opened his door and greeted Rumrill—I mean on that day Rumrill first took the electric train to the old man's house, in anticipation, like yourselves, of a job interview—Brocklebank had already managed to forget that he and I were practically strangers, at most acquaintances, "chums," condescension expressed by each in his way and misunderstood by each to be solicitude, and so welcomed me as though this was a job I had already done for him on many occasions in the past.

He added: As though this was not in reality my debut at *Schloss* Brocklebank.

Rumrill said: I'm sure you'll agree that to forget the face or voice of a close friend is no great feat compared to the achievement of forgetting the strangeness of a stranger. I'm sure you'll agree that to consign an absence to oblivion must be the result of an exceptional variety of genius.

He added: Or illness.

Rumrill said: Not only did this senile old Austrian man believe me to have sat his cats a number of times in the past, he believed as well that I'd already worked as his amanuensis and so had transcribed or taken dictation and then typed up the very instructions to which I was now to refer—though surely I wouldn't need them, expert that I was—while I watched over Brocklebank's presumably beloved animals numbers one through thirty. He wore a wool hat and sweater-vest, both maroon, in the swimming heat of the season, when out the door he walked at last with suitcase or perhaps valise.

He added: Out of his goddamn mind, in other words.

Brocklebank writes: Inclining toward a view where cat-fancying has a causative effect on human relationships, instead of simply being a symptom.

Rumrill said: He didn't have a phone, that Brocklebank. While I was at his house, while he was away, no one could reach me.

He added: Not that I need have worried.

Rumrill said: I couldn't imagine anyone who might have needed to reach me, but had the occasion arisen, it would have proved impossible. I couldn't imagine anyone who might *desire* to reach me, but had the occasion arisen, it would have proved impossible.

He added: Word of flood and famine frustrated.

Rumrill said: Firstly, whoever had targeted Rumrill in this way would have needed to *find* the house, and then of course it would have been up to me whether or not to answer the door. Had I decided in the negative, these Samaritans would have been obliged to throw gravel at the second-floor windows to get my attention, and then, in the stillness, self-conscious, exposed to the suspicions of passersby, they would have needed to test the first-floor windows to see if these were unlocked.

He added: No dice.

Rumrill said: If I decide to hire you, and you'd like to disconnect my phone to simulate this experience, I hope you'll feel free. You'll find the street-noise doesn't come in at all.

He added: Consider this house a stronghold.

Brocklebank writes: Never finding it interesting, tinkering with gears; forcing myself to sit for lessons for almost six weeks and my father never thinking I practiced enough and so firing the teacher; it was true, I wasn't interested in practicing, I probably wasn't interested in the ticking I went on to make.

Rumrill said: Well you might ask, additionally, why it was I would prolong my time away from home, in Brocklebank's house, when I am so disinclined, as previously mentioned, to leave my own modest domicile, and given the aforesaid flimsiness of the time spent outside it, unprotected by its familiarities. I might answer that, in those days, when I still lived surrounded by neighbors and neighbors' balconies, there was something about the old man's house that fascinated me, in preference to my own—something I would be forced to call its superior substantiality, its solid presence and persistence in my mind even when I was away from it, even when I was in my own home, admittedly in those days provisional and imperfect, but which I had tried so often and taken such pains to fix properly in my memory, to make solid, so as to ameliorate the anxiety I felt upon leaving its flimsy shores (and thus my flimsy habits, and thus my flimsy character) unprotected by my presence, and vice versa.

He added: Brocklebank and his history, Brocklebank and his house, Brocklebank and his menagerie somehow more ancient, more appropriate, more predicative, more significant, more isolated from the big world around it.

Brocklebank writes: My wife telling me that America had corrupted me, with which I agree.

Rumrill said: Indeed, were I to hire you, when you yourselves come back from a long day hard at whatever work it is that you do, and walk in the front door of *this* house, and are assailed by its atmosphere, by its geography, by the low wattage of my bulbs, you may find, as I did, that the continuity of your time here with my cats edges out the continuity of whatever you do outside. You may find that even the physical evidence of your activities outside of my house lack a certain substantiality in the face of your duties here.

He added: Consider this house a stronghold.

Rumrill said: This state is, believe me, far preferable to its obverse, or do I mean inverse, by which malady I have been crippled for most of my life. I mean an anxiety regarding the substantiality of those places in which one feels nominally safe on those occasions one must leave them; I mean the fear, when one is out in the big world, away from one's home, that that home and those parts of it which have become most familiar or comforting, or in any case emblematic of its atmosphere, have somehow ceased.

He added: Sunk.

Rumrill said: It may be that you have no sympathy for that kind of distress, since the annihilation of your own home would be cause only for celebration, probably for yourselves as much as those few of our townspeople who can still remember what life here was like before their construction. You will have to take my word that this fear is a terrible thing.

He added: Crippling.

Rumrill said: You will have to take my word that this fear has terrible consequences. You will have to take it as read that it is horrible to depart from one's home and believe that in one's absence it has no more form than an asymmetrical half-line in a piece of forgotten Middle English verse.

He added: Neglected even by our most respected philologists.

Rumrill said: Such journeys meant for me, despite their likely brevity, a putatively permanent farewell to all the things I held most dear, secret or otherwise—an oddity or illness that might explain my aforementioned reluctance to venture out, which was if anything *more* pronounced in the days before I had a home worthy of the name, when I still worked at the library, in the days before I first made my arrangement with Brocklebank to live what I will not glorify with the term "double life." It did little good to say to myself, as I always did, that what felt like a permanent, irreversible good-bye to my home was no more permanent or irreversible or anxious a *Lebewohl* than that one bids to one's bedroom when one closes one's eyes before sleep, or that one bids to the sun when it sets, or that one bids to a friend when she runs to the toilet, or that one bids to a mouthful of food when one swallows it, or that one bids to the words of a book of Middle English verse when one closes its cover.

He added: Though, come to think of it, why not?

Rumrill said: This sense that only my presence and first-hand perception could protect my home from nonexistence wasn't restricted to my dwelling place, but extended to any locations and landscapes I was likely to occupy or traverse. The difference was that despite the inconvenience and distress I'd be caused by the cessation of say the post office or the grocery store, or, in the era now under discussion, the train station or the library, when I felt such places cease behind me as I turned away and then walked or else was conveyed to a point where I could no longer see them, I felt no regrets at the effacement of these locations with my inattention, however much I might "in my heart" have harbored for them a sentimental attachment.

He added: Thanks to the accumulation of pleasant or even unpleasant memories I might associate with them, such as a blowjob in the library stacks by someone who really knew her business.

Brocklebank writes: Waking at last on the morning of the first of August 1964 I suddenly became aware of the fact that I had dreamed the complete course of this and other systems and to an incredibly detailed degree.

Rumrill said: Brocklebank left town often during the early days of our association, to go I knew not where. I became comprehensively familiar with his house, and what it contained.

He added: So much more realistic than mine.

Rumrill said: I mean that his house was filled with evidence suggesting that Brocklebank had lived a certain number of years and done such things as might lead to the acquisition of whatever objects would best serve to confirm and make plausible his passage through the big world outside its walls. These objects must have led Young Rumrill to make assumptions concerning Brocklebank's presumably cosmopolitan character, conclusions that Young Rumrill then applied to such conversations with his employer as could not be avoided in the transaction of their business, and so saw confirmed or else contradicted.

He added: With carbon copies on pink onionskin.

Rumrill said: I would not have been able to articulate it at the time, but it might be that I envied Brocklebank the credibility he seemed to wield in the world, and the ease with which he could pass through its borders. Though I was not to envy it long.

He added: Given its subsequent collapse.

Rumrill said: Eventually, my supervisor—the woman with whom I went into the stacks most days of the week—resigned her position at the library and moved away from our town. I resigned my own, subordinate position thereafter, though I did so only after a significant enough period of time had passed that no one might think that the one event could have been precipitated by the other.

He added: Causality.

Rumrill said: I remember, on my last day at the library, that I saw a man outside dressed in a hodge-podge of clothing, as a vagrant might, though well-layered and warm, and equipped with cap and backpack. He stooped over a round latticed sewer grate and rolled up a piece of paper he'd been carrying, which even from a distance I could see bore a curious symbol or letter in gold.

He added: Or, anyway, had been written on.

Rumrill said: I walked home from the library on my last day, after my resignation in favor of my Brocklebankian duties, without the feelings of sadness I'd thought I would experience on the occasion. I reasoned away this absence of affect with the explanation that since my work and my daily routine in toto had remained essentially the same throughout my tenure at the library, the matter that would have given my memory a sense that any time had passed—would have given it texture, as it were—was absent from my archives. Which is to say, I might as well have spent only a single day at work there, since all my days at work were substantially the same day.

He added: The same commute, same lunch-break orgasm, same shoes and sandwich.

Brocklebank writes: Using the descriptor "dreamed" belies the understatement and economy of my vision.

Rumrill said: I have learned from my cats'

resistance to change as well as my rigorous auto-observation that the mammalian mind draws correspondences between similarities more than it catalogues differences. Differences cause dissonance, while what the mind most looks forward to is the moment when it can declare that whatever phenomena under observation will continue to behave in the manner the mind has until that moment observed it.

He added: And then wander.

Rumrill said: The mind most desires to achieve the state wherein it is no longer obliged to expend its attention on a given phenomenon. New phenomena, like Mr. and Mrs. Pickles, for example, are irritants, interruptions in the mind's repose—or its self-regard—and, as such, it would like to process these as quickly as possible: overeager to assume that it has reached this moment of sufficient observation, overeager to disregard or otherwise incorporate dissonances into a coherent and therefore ignorable whole.

He added: What bliss.

Rumrill said: I find I can't remember my coworkers' names, or their faces, or their demeanor or habits or manners of speech, save those of the woman in the stacks, and even she has become somewhat bleached. I couldn't even tell you how many people there were, in total, employed at the library.

He added: Probably a number between four and ten.

Rumrill said: I do remember that the man who might have been a vagrant, wearing his warm clothes, rolled his piece of paper into a tube. Thus compacted, he was able to stick it down into the sewer grating, and underground.

He added: Into the town under our town.

Rumrill said: The man who might have been a vagrant walked away very nonchalantly. I was struck, at the time, by the peculiarity of his behavior, and wondered at its significance, and his lack of concern.

He added: All too clear to me now.

Brocklebank writes: Writing it down in the next instance from July 17 to September 4, 1971, only knowing everything that one can hear and see in it, functioning more as a medium, dreaming everything, a sort of violet fog-mist rising between my cats.

Rumrill said: Of course, my days now are all just as indistinguishable as they were then, or had become, after several years of employment at the library. My days now resemble each other much more, in fact, than my days did while I was employed at the library, since I was then obliged at moments within the otherwise compressed and now irretrievable span of time I spent on the payroll to enter donated books into the master catalog, or even the occasional purchase, on the rare occasions our budget allowed this, which is to say that life at the library contained so many more variables than life with my cats, even if these mutable elements were only the titles and subject manner of our acquisitions.

He added: Usually survival manuals or histories of antinomian religious movements, for some reason.

Rumrill said: When I worked at the library, however, I tried always to *dispose* of my time as much as possible. My primary concerns at the library, then, were compression and forgetfulness.

He added: To make the time before and then the time after the lunch break pass as quickly as possible.

Rumrill said: Today, after so many years of this acceleration of my rate of passage through my daylight hours, I am forced, given their relative scarcity, as well as finitude, to do my best to try and conserve them. I would like to apply the brakes.

He added: As it were.

Rumrill said: A vessel as ponderous as myself, however, once a certain velocity has been attained, can't be slowed, turned, or stopped without considerable effort. A vessel as ponderous as myself might take years to slow, turn, or stop.

He added: And so be carried along by its own momentum until it runs out of track, or ocean, or road.

Rumrill said: Panicked, I began to worry, some years ago, at the height of my record-mania, whether it might take as long to relearn how to pay attention to my life as it had been to learn to stop. Though now that I come to say it, it seems only reasonable that this be the case.

He added: Apparently it helps to talk things out.

Rumrill said: If there is a difference between my time now—recordless, aged, equipped with twenty cats and prospectively a nubile if pungent pair of menials—and my time at the library—a callow, youngish shelf-reader, regularly serviced—it is that I now grasp at every exception and anomaly that might distinguish my present-day days, desperate to use them as ballast. Inasmuch, I mean, as I can be certain that I didn't dream them.

He added: Which certainty is hard to come by.

Rumrill said: Particularly because, in spite of the numerous states of mind and even sensations that occur in dreams and of which it is commonly said that they are too private or alien to describe, I find that my own dreams are disappointingly mundane and no less likely to become a gray porridge unworthy of commentary than the events of my days or nights awake. One can dream that one has become an animal, or another person, or, I'm sure, some form of plant life, or even, why not, something entirely inanimate, perhaps a statue or a lamp, a statue or lamp in a bedroom, a statue or lamp forced to observe your sterile wife up to something you'd rather not see, something with another man, or—what's to prevent her—men; but not, I lament, that one has become the color red, for example, or the smell of mildew, or a hapax legomenon, or Analytical Marxism.

He added: Anyway, *I* can't.

Rumrill said: Which means that, night after night, I am condemned to dream as usual of being an animal whose characteristics (inasmuch as they are clear to me) do not differ in any respect from the animal I am obliged to be in the hours I share awake—most equitably, I'd say—with animals such as yourself. You may of course retort that the scenarios in which this dream-animal finds itself embroiled are not themselves likely to occur in my hours awake, but I would reply that this is a poor substitute for the privilege of a nightly soak in an honestly variant, honestly alien, honestly antinomian, sort of logic.

He added: *A Treatise on the Incubus, or Nightmare, Disturbed Sleep, Terrific Dreams, and Nocturnal Visions, with the Means of Removing these Distressing Complaints*, by the Reverend Joseph M. Rumrill, SJ.

Rumrill said: Even erotic thoughts have become difficult for me to utilize as a hypnotic, in those moments before sleep, or meant to precede sleep, since most of what I remember of my romantic life, such as it was, is now quite useless to me, or in any event unwieldy. Each available scenario is linked by ineluctable chains of association to unpleasant memories whose arrival at the fore of what I am pleased to call my mind would only serve to upset me and return me to a state of wakefulness.

He added: What a pisser.

Brocklebank writes: Being unable to speak freely about it, not having an objective relation to it, simply dreaming it thus, next time in the night from December 9 to December 10.

Rumrill said: I have found that I can in a superficial way explain the restraints I impose upon my character when I dream by way of the recollection that I tend to fall asleep having engaged myself in a conversation on a certain subject. This subject often being women, or something I have read or seen or done and now regret.

He added: The silent scurry of my thoughts, with the occasional audible neigh if I become particularly passionate.

Rumrill said: At some point during this conversation, which may become more rational or less by turns as I doze or fail to doze, the paths my dream may take become delineated inadvertently by whatever it is I ruminate upon in my self-address. I am not presented with a choice as to what I may dream about, but what I dream about is necessarily dictated by the terms of this conversation.

He added: A struggle not to use the term "interior monologue."

Rumrill said: In last night's dream, for example, which I have decided represents a learned though cryptic commentary upon our immediate futures, Mister and Missus P., I found myself in the role of the Queen of England. I felt uncomfortable in my dress, and acutely aware of my body.

He added: Or, rather, I felt the awareness of this awareness.

Rumrill said: As the Queen, I wish I could be someone else, some*where* else. As the Queen, I wish to be somewhere else, dressed differently.

He added: An imposter?

Rumrill said: I am anxious, in my dream. In my dream, I am not at all royal.

He added: Thus, a dream about *pretending* to be the Queen of England.

Rumrill said: The Queen or false queen is in a restaurant—I retain the impression that the backs of the chairs are a substance like ivory, voluted with ostentatious swirls and eddies. Still, the food there is no good.

He added: The question of taste in dreams.

Rumrill said: The waiters are deferential, because recruited—I do not deceive myself—from who knows what comedies enjoyed I suppose on the stage, for I have never once been treated with such courtesy under the clammy light of the big world. These waiters or actors as waiters want me to enjoy myself, entirely fooled by my disguise.

He added: As I am not by theirs.

Rumrill said: I invite a sturdy one to sit with me when the bland but bitter meal has ostensibly been consumed. Whether because it is something that I actually want, or because my waiter suggests it, I go on to order a bottle of champagne.

He added: Though to say that one thing happened after another precisely is a misrepresentation.

Rumrill said: As for the Queen's champagne, we drink it together, the waiter and I. It tastes just the same as everything else they've served me.

He added: The uniform taste of dreams.

Brocklebank writes: And so, regarding literary form, though loosely joined together, these notes are, in reality, the outcome of convictions long held and slowly matured.

Rumrill said: Whether or not I was really meant to be the Queen of England in my dream, or was meant instead to be someone who had for whatever reason decided to *impersonate* the Queen, a case could be made that every role taken in a dream is necessarily an imposture. This would include the role of oneself.

He added: No applause, please.

Rumrill said: By "meant," I can only mean "meant by the dreamer." I probably need not tell you that I don't really know what I "meant" by putting myself in drag.

He added: If royal drag.

Rumrill said: We can probably agree that in a dream we are not subject to the same habits, memories, or limitations as when awake, and often find ourselves freighted with behaviors that are inexplicable to our daylight minds. What we often say is that, at the time, we did not question them, odd as they appear by daylight.

He added: Or with eyes open.

Rumrill said: I maintain therefore that my night as the Queen of England, or someone posing as the Queen of England, couldn't really be called interesting, couldn't really be considered "of note," because I remember that it didn't feel out of the ordinary to me at the time. By implication, my thoughts had brought themselves to a point where this scenario was only natural.

He added: As natural as *yumuşak ge* follows *ge*.

Rumrill said: A dream that surprised me entirely would have to be characterized as a nightmare. This would be a dream that forced me to breathe an entirely foreign air.

He added: Cold and probably thin.

Brocklebank writes: Insisting on stimulating activity.

Rumrill said: Even in a dream, you know, friendliness has its limits, and soon my waiter gets up to bring me the bill. I am aghast at the figure when I see it.

He added: Despite its fairness.

Rumrill said: Not that I can claim to have seen any real number at all. It was only the impression of a number, the shape of one.

He added: An ideogram?

Rumrill said: The Queen's bill, written on paper from a modern, green-shaded accountant's pad, lined in red, was the manifestation of an imperative, directed to me, the protagonist of my dream, by the scenarist of my dream—an imperative that I could neither under-stand nor endorse. Why would I want to put myself in this position?

He added: Again.

Rumrill said: The logic of the dream demands that I be anxious now. I don't want to be found out.

He added: And humiliated.

Brocklebank writes: Such concentration only being possible in the absence of self-pity.

Rumrill said: I can't recall offhand where I came across the phrase "ineluctable chains of association," though I'm positive these words are in my head because they struck me as especially pleasing or especially tire-some when I first happened upon their use, or a quota-tion thereof, or an inadvertent coinage after the fact by someone who had themselves come upon the phrase in one or another form, finding it pleasing or tiresome, and so forth. The awareness that virtually every phrase in one's head has the same or a similar genealogy—though naturally some more than others announce themselves as hand-me-downs—is a condition I find repellent.

He added: And for which our dreams offer no balm.

Rumrill said: It is likewise repellent that exaspera-tion is as likely as enjoyment to impress itself upon our memory; indeed, that disgust results in the most ined-ible impressions. I can't recall offhand where I came across the phrase "ineluctable chains of association," but how well I remember, by contrast, where and when I first saw Old Man Brocklebank, in particular because of his partiality to odiously bright colors (because lower chromatic values could no longer pierce the milk-fog over his corneas?), in particular because he found it needful to be at every hour a prismatic battlefield whose noisome ferocity could not help but draw the eyes of every civilian unhappily caught up in the fray.

He added: And, on the subject of disgust, that weird little bulge near what might have been his kidneys.

Rumrill said: Brocklebank's bulge baffled me entirely, throughout the years of our association. Was Brocklebank squeezed into some kind of girdle underneath his shirt?

He added: But he was such a skinny man.

Rumrill said: I longed to give it a good poke. I longed to see, for example, if it would scuttle away.

He added: And if the old man would even notice.

Rumrill said: "Longed" is an overstatement. It would be more accurate to say that I thought of this poke with a certain regularity, for example when, as his caretaker, I was obliged to put Mr. Brocklebank to bed.

He added: Well satisfied with his day, snug in his canary-yellow woolen nightshirt.

Brocklebank writes: Subsisting only as administered practice of a tautological exercise devoid of inner necessity.

Rumrill said: Well you might ask, as concerns Misters Brocklebank and Rumrill, "Why cats, specifically?" And I would answer, for one, "They don't need to go outside."

He added: Re: the phenomena of substitution for one's own et cetera.

Rumrill said: Well you might proceed to ask, "So, why not fish or birds?" And I would answer, "Perhaps cats are at home in houses in a way that those animals aren't."

He added: Less captive.

Rumrill said: For a cat, the interior of a house is a substitute for the big world beyond its walls. For a cat, houses contain their own geography, wild game, weather, natural disasters; and inside our houses they have the privilege of perambulation say upstairs and down and really to any point on the compass.

He added: More themselves out of the big world than in it.

Brocklebank writes: Preferring to think of my system as a sort of natural phenomenon—something that has always been present in ordinary home life, and which I simply observed, rather than invented.

Rumrill said: Initially, when he was still able to leave his house, and his memory was only given to the occasional hiccup, I was only needed to do the old man the occasional favor. But then his tremors, and his arthritis, and with them his disinclination to go out, and with it his forgetfulness, all began to advance at a more than casual rate.

He added: Unless it was his forgetfulness first, and with *it* his disinclination, and with *it* his et cetera.

Rumrill said: Since he would have needed a functional memory in order for the deterioration of his memory to be clear to him, it cannot have been a gradual comprehension of his own vulnerability that led Brocklebank by and by to become reluctant to the point of truculence when confronted by the threat of a jaunt out of doors. It could not have been comprehension of his own vulnerability and along with it the concurrent inflation of what we might call his conjectural faculty with regard to all the likely dangers awaiting him in the open air.

He added: E.g., fire and flood, armed insurgents, what have you.

Rumrill said: Why then I so insisted on his daily constitutional when I became his de facto nurse, I cannot surmise. One would think that Rumrill of all people would have had sympathy for the old man's reluctance to leave base.

He added: Crippled by analogous anxieties.

Rumrill said: It could have been on the orders of our town doctor, who, after his failure to keep Mrs. Brocklebank among the quick, was I imagine doubly intent on the prolongation of Mr. Brocklebank's torments, and who thus prescribed regular exercise as a supplement to the old man's baffling regimen of pills, powders, and gels. Or perhaps it was simply that one has little patience when forced to observe one's own weaknesses parodied in the person of a fellow citizen.

He added: Of inferior quality.

Brocklebank writes: The hope being to induce the experience of the general form from a sufficiently dense superimposition of specifics.

Rumrill said: For example, it takes no great effort to imagine a comely and immodestly attired woman on parade down one of the streets in our town's summertime. She is elegant as she deflects a stream of fruity cicada piss from her hair and eyes by means of a folded early edition of our local newspaper.

He added: Purchased at the nearby neighborhood grocery.

Rumrill said: Further, it takes no great effort to

imagine Mr. Pickles, alone on one of his own healthful constitutionals, on a street perpendicular to our subject, his lungs filled with heavy air, symptom of a black storm cloud that will soon stretch itself across our sky with a clap of et cetera. He sees this woman, perhaps on her lunch break from the library, and he has the luck to be unobserved while engaged in this inspection of his fellow citizen, well within his legal rights and unlikely to have consequences.

He added: Unlikely even to occupy a place in the memory.

Rumrill said: Until, that is, he "catches a glimpse," thanks to a movement in his peripheral vision, of another mister, let us say seated at an outdoor café, of which at this time there were still one or two in our town. He is no danger to virile Mr. P., this fellow, but it cannot be denied that his presence puts your husband, madam, on guard; while the man too is now on his alert, not on account of Mr. Pickles, who remains unnoticed, but because of the approach of said comely et cetera, whose trajectory puts her on a direct course to his place at the café.

He added: The vertex of the angle created by the intersection of lines W and P.

Rumrill said: This comrade of Pickles is a fellow inspector of woman. This comrade of Pickles sits with a cigarette clutched feasibly between his lips, and with his pant legs raised to show white socks with green stripes tugged all the way to where his disagreeable calves become two gray and extravagant knees.

He added: An outrageous leer on his puss.

Rumrill said: To catch sight of such a man, as

your husband has now done, dear lady, in this parable—a man likewise engaged in the immodest perception of our ostensibly immodest woman—is to have
one's own ogle ruined, cheapened. Mr. P. has been
made to feel more vulnerable, isolated, scrutinized in
his observation than had he himself been "caught in
the act" by a third party.

He added: Perhaps you, mournful Missus.

Rumrill said: This because he has seen himself
depicted in the person of that barefaced birdwatcher.
He has seen his own behavior portrayed thereupon as,
variously, base, obvious, grotesque.

He added: As amateur street theater.

Rumrill said: Additionally, and for no extra
charge, we might imagine that this other man, this
travesty of Pickles, might soon be joined—albeit
unnoticed, in turn, by himself—by the woman to
whom he is in reality attached, wedded, obligated.
He has been caught unawares by his own wife in this
attitude of impotent lasciviousness.

He added: Pickles the only unperceived perceiver in this quadrilateral.

Rumrill said: Mr. P. watches the wife observe the
husband eye the woman dressed perhaps imprudently
on this sunny or soon sunless day in the rainy season. And our original woman, as she walks, is now
unable to avoid or ignore the sight of her two principal observers, male and female, at the outdoor café, so
blatant is their double regard.

He added: She the caboose in this milk train of
the gaze.

Rumrill said: For a moment, then, she is united

with the unseen Mr. P., who is gifted on this day with an uncharacteristic perspicacity, in a shared curiosity as to what it was that could have yoked to one another these two unhappy individuals, male and female, these two beacons of discontent. What, that is, could have caused this particular woman of all the women in our historic town to look upon the gawp or gape of this particular man and say, "I could do worse"?

He added: And by extension, poor Mr. P., your own wife vis-à-vis yourself?

Brocklebank writes: Believing that the absolute formality of my system touches in us a fact that is as deep as our humanity: the fact is that everything in our speech and in our thinking is elaborately organized.

Rumrill said: Or else, if you'd prefer a more sentimental scenario, it takes not much more effort to pluck Mr. P. from this scene in our town center and deliver him to one on its periphery, out where our sovereign thoroughfares become unreconstructed plain. He is cast on this occasion as an old man's caregiver.

He added: Not implausible.

Rumrill said: In the room in our town's hospital where men and women were once wheeled to die, he stands to the side, does our hero, in his professional capacity. Let's face it, a job's a job, and even with those damp, sickly rats in its lobby, the bank does still expect your payments to be regular.

He added: I assume.

Rumrill said: There are ridges and canyons in the lime-washed brick walls that are the room's only decoration. The light through the cantilevered and mesh-netted windows is the color of a fly's wing.

He added: Good, plausible details.

Rumrill said: Mr. P. has accompanied his old man to the hospital on this day, not because the old man is dying—he won't go so peacefully!—but because his (the old man's) wife will not live much longer. This old man and woman have no children, and so are attended in extremis not by sons or son's daughters and daughters or daughter's sons, but by this paid amanuensis, nursemaid.

He added: Which is to say, in this scenario, Mr. Pickles.

Rumrill said: Mr. P. is forced, now, to watch the old man watch the old woman gasp her last. In her, Mr. P. sees his own inevitable frailty, and in the old man, his own future dissolution, for the old man is no more attentive to his wife than would be a nameless cat, and no more capable of grief; his memory undermined, gobbled up, oblivionated by diseases of his own.

He added: What a pisser.

Rumrill said: That is, in the old man, who perhaps owns a great many housecats, or will soon acquire them, once he's a widower, Mr. P. sees an inevitability no less somber than the grave: the breakdown of all the systems that constitute the orderly function of his mind, its patterns and preferences, its sovereign thoroughfares. While in parallel, or perhaps in contrast, or perhaps just "cruelly," Mr. P. sees that the old man's sterile wife is no less coherent and aware in extremis, despite her age and illnesses, than she was when she first met her future widower on the front steps of the Österreichische Nationalbibliothek.

He added: If it has front steps.

Rumrill said: But each of our three imaginary watchers—the healthy man, the near-death but cogent woman, and the less-near-death but doolally old fellow—share the same fundamental reaction to this awesome, supreme moment; which is to say that they are bored, so awfully and profoundly bored, just horribly scourged by tedium. All three want to get away, want it all over with, want the old barren lady to pass out or away.

He added: Want all visitors shooed from the ward.

Rumrill said: And, as in our sexier scenario, though no one is mindful of his presence, no one remembers he's there, poor Mr. Pickles finds himself all the more exposed to *his own* scrutiny thanks to this practical invisibility. Mr. P. sees his own merciless self-indulgence, his desire to escape responsibility, adulthood, sentience, made manifest on the faces of the old man and woman, and is ashamed.

He added: At this vaudeville of his basest nature.

Brocklebank writes: Lofty ambitions of fame having long faded, the challenge excessiveness presents to daily coherence remains viable and exciting, especially when expressed within the confines of a well-structured but indescribable aesthetic.

Rumrill said: Which is why I'm delighted, by the way, to see how little you both resemble *me*, tangibly or in-; how little I can find even a hint of my own ignobility in your eyes, voices, comportment. Even the grossest and most offensive caricaturist would be obliged to confess that of my quintessence you partake not at all.

He added: Wet from the big, inclement out-of-doors.

Rumrill said: Nor would he or I find ourselves tempted even for a moment to inquire how it is two such specimens as yourselves might have married. Nor indeed inquire how it is you found yourselves drawn or corralled into our soggy little town.

He added: Spit and image, as you are, of each other, and of it.

Rumrill said: Indeed, it's on the basis of our non-resemblance, Rumrill to Pickles, that I feel our arrangement might have what is called a future. It's on the basis of our non-resemblance that I am most intrigued by the question of whether you might in time prove receptive to the sights and sensations and so thoughts that would hem you in, here, in my home.

He added: Hem you in, I mean, to your betterment.

Brocklebank writes: Discovering that cat-fancying *in itself* can be a totally plastic phenomenon, suggesting its own shape, design, and poetic metaphor.

Rumrill said: But yes, he was a sick, sentimental, senile old Austrian man. I continue to refer to Brocklebank.

He added: *Primum movens.*

Rumrill said: I am well aware that, apart from the word "Austrian," such a description could well refer to myself. One day you might yourselves refer to me just so to your friends or coworkers: "Once we pet-sat twenty cats, owned by a sick, sentimental, senile old townie."

He added: Insofar as anything I might say would

still be recognizable, repeated in the language of *Homo cucumis*.

Rumrill said: This particular sick, sentimental, senile old Austrian man had been employed in the capacity of watch and clock repairman for nearly fifty years. Soon after he met and employed me first as cat-sitter and eventually less-than-nubile amanuensis, his stiff and outraged hands began to shake so often and in their tremors describe such wide parabola that the only watch Brocklebank could have repaired safely would have had a radius of no less than eight meters.

He added: Property of a client no doubt accustomed to getting his way.

Rumrill said: Brocklebank and his sterile wife had moved to our town some years ago. They had given up a rent-controlled apartment in Greenwich Village, some ways from our little town, which (our historic town) must have seemed so full of charm, so empty of threats, by contrast, aside from those threats that might be classified as metaphysical, and of course the occasional fearsome cabal of metalworkers or firemen or Pullman-car constructors.

He added: Albeit more disputatious than violent.

Rumrill said: Brocklebank had decided to give up his apartment in order to be with his sterile wife unmolested by the world that had already disappointed them at length and with great resourcefulness. Brocklebank had decided to give his apartment up in order to be in his decline surrounded by the quaintness and rustic character our town and neighborhood were no doubt famous for in the days when word of such things traveled quickly.

He added: Out of his goddamn mind, in other words.

Brocklebank writes: And being reluctant to endorse the superficial headlines of newspapers.

Rumrill said: Toward the end of Brocklebank's life there wasn't much he could do on his own save complain. Already his sometime employee, I was eventually recruited to help him do everything except complain.

He added: Until at last recruited to do even this.

Rumrill said: I could hardly complain on my own behalf that I had been thus coopted, as in those days I didn't have much else to occupy me, save a day job that had long since ceased to be of interest. Oddly, now that I have nothing at all to occupy me, I find myself occupied entirely.

He added: At war with the present participle.

Rumrill said: I fought for a long while to avoid the role of live-in caregiver. Even with my perhaps suspicious abundance of leisure time, outside of my daily, minimally remunerative hours at the town library—I mean when hired initially as a simple cat-sitter, in the days when Brocklebank was still mobile and still fond of travel, or so he claimed—even with nowhere else to go but back to the brick building I then shared with men and women who spoke about me in muted, amused tones whenever I happened to pass them on the way to or from my mailbox; even with little more to concern me than my daily assignations with my supervisor against the starry backdrop of standardized bindings whose gilt letters had been worn off by generations of unchaste librarians not unlike ourselves; even in such bleak circumstances I considered it "too much" for my employer to demand that I remain inside of his oppressively plausible home night after night to earn the money I had agreed to accept in return for the careful maintenance of his cats.

He added: With, I am assured, at least a soupçon of sincerity.

Rumrill said: It seemed unnecessary for me to be over-solicitous in my care for the thirty animals I had been paid to feed and conserve. It seemed unnecessary for me to be over-solicitous in *any* task I had been set.

He added: By some senile old Austrian.

Rumrill said: I persisted in my inattention though I knew that Brocklebank's menagerie constituted said senile old Austrian man's primary raison d'être, or do I mean symptom. Brocklebank's wife had been dead at this point for some time, although no greater a span than you would consider unlikely, and so his diminished capacities had little else to occupy them.

He added: Mrs. Brocklebank's eyes probably nothing like the sun.

Brocklebank writes: People having every reason, then, to ask, "Is your system good for me if I don't like or enjoy it?"

Rumrill said: In my defense, Brocklebank's animals were not very social organisms. They preferred to hide from their caretaker when in the front door he walked, his facetious human throat and tongue alive with the language of his fathers.

He added: To wit, "Time for din-dins!"

Rumrill said: What did it profit Rumrill to track the old man's cats to their hidey-holes in the vents and beneath the furniture or baseboards and in the closets and behind the paintings to make certain they were alive and happy? Brocklebank who couldn't even remember that he and I were virtual strangers could hardly be counted on to know the difference between a contented cat and a despondent one, or even thirty cats from twenty-nine, or twenty-eight, or six, or three.

He added: *A Liturgy of Feline Funerary Offerings in the Egyptian Predynastic Period*, by Sir E. A. Thompson Rumrill.

Rumrill said: I will now tell you the story of my first week entrusted with Brocklebank's animals, a source of no little shame for your prospective employer, if you're familiar with the concept of "shame"; it will stand as a cautionary tale, and you might yourselves want to repeat it someday, for example in case you need a breather while I'm away and take it into your heads to invite a sub-cat-sitter to take your places; or indeed to whomever you will in time ask to take care of your own home, wherever that might be, should you ever manage, I mean, to escape your current place of residence, with that cheap, poisonous insulation stuffed into its walls, and acquire a house of your own, filled with cats of your own, or perhaps some other form of livestock. You can tell the story, and perhaps even make use of what remains of these notes when I've moved on—such an ambiguous phrase—to provide illustrative detail for this cautionary tale; or, why not, your own notes, typed up when our interview is over, based upon your dim memories of my filibuster here in the foyer; it takes no great effort to imagine the clatter of keys in the dim light of your habitat, the impress of your words, ill chosen, from your meager stock, onto soggy paper stolen from some defunct stationer, which goes squish with every typebar swoop:

notes taken on my notes, in your debased argot, pretty much incomprehensible to a man of my generation, but I commend your actions, for we must take into account the likelihood that my own dossier on the subject, the size of a book, or my years of records, now stored in Brocklebank's hand-me-down cabinets, will not survive intact my perchance prolonged absence; despite my precautions, despite their (the cabinets') advertised resistance to fire and flood.

He added: And earthquakes and parataxis.

Rumrill said: It was only a day or two before Brocklebank's scheduled return from that first trip that Rumrill asked himself if he'd seen even a single cat in his tenure as sitter. He found himself unable to reply with any certainty.

He added: Consternation.

Rumrill said: Surely the amounts of food and water left in the many bowls, say three bowls per floor, should have served as evidence either for or against the continued health or indeed existence of the cats in Brocklebank's home? Surely the excrement trawled from the many litter boxes should likewise have served as evidence?

He added: Surely.

Rumrill said: Young Rumrill had not been careful enough with regard to his responsibilities; he had neither filled nor emptied enough of the bowls or boxes to have proof positive of the existence of life in Brocklebank's house. Looking at a given bowl or box, Young Rumrill saw that he could argue either pro or contra and find either argument substantiated by the evidence, or lack of evidence.

He added: No easy matter to differentiate between old and new food or shit or water.

Rumrill said: That Young Rumrill hadn't visited the house on a daily basis, or been especially methodical on those days he did bother to stop by, only served to confuse matters further. He had attended to certain floors on certain of the days he'd thought to visit and neglected others on others, rather than see to each and every station on every single day of Brocklebank's junket, as he'd promised.

He added: Without method and so without memory of which bowls or boxes had been attended to and when.

Rumrill said: The book-length series of typed notes given to me by Brocklebank contained instructions as to which bowls or boxes should be filled or emptied at which times—on which days, during which sorts of clear or inclement weather, at what positions of the sun over or beyond our town—for example, from civil to astronomical twilight—in what moods, in what order, and with which hands. If obedience to Brocklebank's system was meant, in Brocklebank's eyes, to achieve a particular effect, Young Rumrill had not had the patience to read a sufficient number of the pages of this poorly typed and occasionally incoherent opus to determine so.

He added: With carbon copies on pink onionskin.

Rumrill said: But this Rumrill was hardly so obtuse as not to recognize that had he bothered to read and follow Brocklebank's instructions, the missing cats would if nothing else be concrete presences, whether healthy or dead or infirm, because dealt with systematically. In retrospect it appeared to this Rumrill that Brocklebank's system was a lifeline that had been extended to him in mute beneficence by the old man, and that he, callow youth, had ignored: a means not necessarily toward whatever esoteric ends Brocklebank had intended, but for the establishment of a basic certitude regarding the existence of thirty cats reluctant to admit to their own materiality.

He added: *Ach so!*

Rumrill said: But suspended as Young Rumrill was on that afternoon before Brocklebank's return—our records indicate it was a Sunday—in all his guilt and uncertainty, Brocklebank's cats were for him a burdensome hypothesis rather than an animal warmth. They were either there and dead, or there and alive, or not there and dead, or not there and alive.

He added: And if there were no cats, we must wonder, was there even a Rumrill to take care of them?

Rumrill said: He opted for an empirical resolution to his dilemma, despite a history of disappointment with this approach. He ransacked the house with his fingers, which were powdered soon with disobliging soot.

He added: Everything found was not a cat.

Rumrill said: Our Rumrill next devised numerous scenarios to justify a disregard for this crisis he had caused. For example, he told himself, Brocklebank had never had any cats, or else these cats had died long ago and the old man had already forgotten.

He added: Forgotten he had no cats in need of a sitter.

Rumrill said: Or else, alternatively, that Brocklebank had owned thirty of some other sort of animal and in his dementia had forgotten which species; as though some ancient Austrian race memory that pertained to urban life in small and shared spaces had confined him to those assumptions proper to the maintenance of a great many housecats, whether or not these assumptions had any relevance to the species of animal he had in fact managed to collect here upon the open and exposed prairie. Perhaps the old man had inadvertently murdered by neglect those animals he'd acquired because he had developed the senile expectation that creatures kept traditionally in cages, for example, would be able despite their incarceration to feed and water and sanitize themselves, on their own recognizance, at the numerous stations provided for these activities.

He added: As would a cat.

Rumrill said: Perhaps Brocklebank had forgotten that these miscellaneous creatures were *not* able to perambulate at will say upstairs and down or really to any point on the compass. Perhaps he had forgotten what sort of animal he had begun to collect after the death of his sterile wife, whether these were parrots or hamsters or Asian carp or bill collectors seeking back rent or local girls who'd had the misfortune to ride past *Burgruine* Brocklebank on their girl-bicycles while he happened to be stationed at the picture window in his study—perhaps, Young Rumrill reasoned, Brocklebank had forgotten that he'd never owned a cat.

He added: And then had forgotten that he'd forgotten.

Rumrill said: These theories comforted Young Rumrill in the candid light of said picture window above Brocklebank's trestle desk and typewriter, but despite their pleasantness it was impossible for him to convince himself, much as he wanted to be convinced, that he was not under threat of exposure as the sort of fellow who would take money from an elderly citizen of our honest town in exchange for the performance of duties then left inexcusably unexecuted or executed so poorly as to leave even parties with a vested interest in his welfare and good name—which is to say, Rumrill—unable to persuade themselves of his innocence. There was no doubt in Rumrill's mind that it would be obvious to any even minimally cognizant Austrian that Rumrill had been a cheat.

He added: A scoundrel, twicer, cad, or bounder.

Rumrill said: In a panic as to the old man's probable reaction to the sight of his house now depopulated of some or all of its thirty probable cats—demand for a refund, if not criminal charges, at the very least a day in small-claims court, a venue from which Rumrill had already been warned to keep his distance in future—the wayward cat-sitter concluded that he needed to replace the animals that he might or might not himself have killed before the old man returned. But where, Rumrill wondered, could one possibly find thirty actual cats to replace thirty likely cats?

He added: In a single night?

Rumrill said: And yet, be not so hasty, Young Rumrill. You could stand to be a little less ambitious.

He added: Always welcome news.

Rumrill said: He didn't need thirty cats; he only needed as many would be necessary to give a minimally cognizant Austrian the *impression* that his house contained thirty cats. There must, Rumrill concluded, be a magic number between five and twenty that would to Brocklebank's unsuspicious eyes be indistinguishable from the full complement.

He added: Crafty Rumrill!

Rumrill said: He could rely on Brocklebank's mistaken memories of their long association to smooth over any likely reservations that might develop as to his culpability should the gaff be, as it were, blown. He could rely on Brocklebank's dementia to smooth over any obvious discrepancies in color, temperament, gender between the newly corralled cats and those he had neglected.

He added: If any.

Rumrill said: Need we say that Young Rumrill set out that evening in hope? Need we say that he was unencumbered by doubt as he walked off over asphalt and concrete?

He added: Not to mention the regular polygons in pitiless green of flowering plants of the family *Poaceae*?

Rumrill said: Not many more hours of discouragement passed than you would find improbable before our lad reached the conclusion that the acquisition of a new harem of cats for my employer in numbers between five and twenty would prove just as impossible as the acquisition of the entire thirty or indeed fifty or seventy-five. Either there were no cats in our town or Rumrill didn't know them when he saw them.

He added: Or else they'd been warned to make themselves scarce.

Rumrill said: It was then that Young Rumrill thought, I think for the first time, of my supervisor, the librarian, the woman in the stacks—the first time, I mean, in that these new thoughts of her were independent of the anticipation or memory of what we did and would continue for some time to do together in the stacks. Specifically, he thought that she might, depending on her character, habits, and degree of familiarity with his town—matters that were, I am ashamed to say, complete mysteries to him then and myself now—know better than a Rumrill of any age where a desperate, failed empiricist might acquire if not a great many then at least a satisfactory number of housecats on what all evidence suggests was a Sunday afternoon.

He added: Soon consumed, as is often the case, by evening of the same day.

Rumrill said: It was always possible, was it not, that the woman in the stacks might have been agreeable to this extension of their relationship from the concrete to the formal stage of development? But this plan progressed no further than its conception, because the first obstacle encountered in its execution was insurmountable: Rumrill didn't know how to contact the woman in the stacks: he didn't know her address, or phone number, or shoe size; though he did, in those days, know her name.

He added: Though not because she'd told him.

Rumrill said: The woman in the stacks had exchanged perhaps three hundred words with Rumrill, if never about what they did together in the stacks. The woman in the stacks would say good-bye to him along with his colleagues at the library every day at an hour when in winter the sun would already be down and in summer the sun would still be in the sky; then she would walk alone or with a female colleague to the nearby underground rail station, there to board the electric train that would transport her back over our town's only bridge—this barely the height of a church steeple, and with no body of water to span save what puddles might have formed between the cars of our famous railway graveyard—to a neighborhood where Rumrill did not live, and would not have been welcome.

He added: For such is the way of things.

Rumrill said: She was a supervisor and had what I suppose would be called "real" responsibilities, whereas I was assigned only menial tasks at the library, things no one else could be bothered with, such as the categorization of new purchases, though my disinterest was such that I filed even murder mysteries under "self-improvement." On occasion too I would be forced to reshelve the books that had been returned to us on time or late by the elderly members of our community, Austrian or otherwise, who were the library's only regular patrons; but when midday arrived, she and I would both, head and hands, abandon our work and slip into the stacks, without a glance in each other's direction, as though each of us had been possessed by no more than an innocent curiosity as to

the characteristic dimensions of a sixth-century narthex, our mutual disinterest upheld until we'd reached
a particular intersection of two narrow passageways
between the rows of metal shelves, infrequently trod,
sheltered and silenced by who knows how many thousands of volumes of partially disintegrated wood pulp,
whose particles spotted our skin and no doubt found
new readers deep in the pink of our lungs.

He added: What the hell is a narthex?

Rumrill said: If Rumrill could have found the
residence of the woman in the stacks, whether her
building was old and squat and snug or new and tall
and damp, would she have put on her red coat and
scarf and walked with Rumrill into the Sunday evening
chill or heat to seek for Brocklebank a new bevy of cats?
Would she have understood the gravity of Rumrill's
dilemma and devoted herself to this pursuit with the
same grim aptitude she brought to those activities she
and he engaged in among books by and large ignored
since before either of them had been—in this town or
elsewhere—born?

He added: Metal shelves bolted with thick blue
zinc-plated cylinders to floor and ceiling.

Rumrill said: Was it wrong of Young Rumrill to
entertain the notion that his coworker—simply on the
basis of her inclination to fuck regularly a colleague
with whom she had shared no more than three hundred innocuous words of what might be called "polite
conversation"—words devoid of any semantic import
above that of a grunt or shrug—might be inclined,
firstly, to help her accomplice and then, into the bar-
gain, been possessed of the necessary wisdom and self-
assurance to go in search of whatever chattel her grateful

subordinate claimed for reasons unknown to be needful? Was it wrong of him to think that she might care to inconvenience herself on his behalf, simply on account of her regular relations with this Rumrill, who in his gratitude or panic never once saw fit to pass the time of day with his colleague, with this woman of women, under circumstances less intimate?

He added: "The time of day"?

Rumrill said: Was he mistaken to assume that said woman of women would even recognize our cat-sitter manqué should he appear on her doorstep? Would she be able to correlate Rumrill's face and figure with the virile member, as I am pleased to call it, of which, once a workday, Monday through Friday, she took time off from her workday to reacquaint herself?

He added: Answer me.

Brocklebank writes: Reaching out through and beyond mankind, trying to see what I can of the infinite and its immensities—throwing back to you whatever I can, but ever conscious that if I would contemplate the greater, I must wrestle with the lesser, even though it dims the outline.

Rumrill said: Humid, oppressive, and interminable in its sympathetic disinclination to become the day of humiliation that would in all likelihood follow, the night in question parted around Rumrill in his catless perambulation to reveal a house not altogether distant from Brocklebank's. This house was singular in that it was no longer fortified with a front lawn whose dominant vegetation belonged in a general way to the family *Poaceae*, but instead with a level plane of gray gravel.

He added: Through the interstices of which the

ancient prairie upon which our town had been founded could already be seen to have reasserted itself in the form of scraggly yellow tendrils.

Rumrill said: Something about this neighborly heresy on a street full of green inclined the seeker to consider the house worth investigation. The door was unlocked, perhaps even ajar, and to Rumrill's mild surprise the smell in the vestibule or foyer was that of a great number of housecats.

He added: When I was scratched, in those days— such blood.

Rumrill said: Unlikely though it sounds, it stands to reason that Rumrill succeeded in his quest to replenish Brocklebank's store of cats; or else that it did not after all need to be replenished, since, for one, when the old man was himself in extremis, at the very end of his Austrian life, I remember that there was still the question of how to dispose of those thirty cats when he finally popped off— which implies that there must, logically, have been thirty cats of which to dispose. It never entered my mind that I should inherit them.

He added: It hadn't occurred to me that I could have any use for them.

Brocklebank writes: Cat-fancying is never innocuous—because it's celebratory.

Rumrill said: You see, so large a number of cats in captivity are never forced to settle in disposition on either extremity of the binary typically available to those species that have thrown in their lot with our doomed human settlements. So large a number of cats could not be described as feral, but neither are they domesticated.

He added: Better said, they are homeowners.

Rumrill said: As Brocklebank's decline was about to reach its nadir, and so deposit him in the ground somewhere in the vicinity of his sterile wife— though not so sterile in death, I presume, now that the waterlogged seedlife of our town could have its way with her—one question was whether Brocklebank's cats could survive on their own, as strays, if released into what I suppose could be called, for convenience's sake, "the wild" after so long a time within Brocklebank's house and fancy. Another question was whether homes could be found for them, in groups or individually, and who would want to take on this responsibility.

He added: The humane society wanted nothing to do with it.

Rumrill said: Another question still was whether it might be a legitimate concern that Brocklebank's cats might haunt me if I was to burn or drown or throttle them, in groups or individually. Was there a threshold—morally, mathematically—beyond which X number of murdered animals might not equal, in the six eyes of the Eumenides, the murder of a human being?

He added: A legitimate concern inasmuch as I might find myself concerned with it.

Rumrill said: Not that I would go on record with the *Pickles Times* to state that it's out of the question that one or more of the cats who now live in my house, or who share it with me, or who are kept here prisoner, is or are remnants of Brocklebank's larger and more theoretically inclined menagerie. Why bother to rule this out?

He added: I do not rule out.

Brocklebank writes: Cat-fancying being a system, considering one's animals not as living beings with a birth, lifetime, and death, but as objects that can be easily and arbitrarily permutated in all directions.

Rumrill said: Come to think of it, Brocklebank didn't really name his thirty cats so much as prepare a *list* of names to apply to whichever constituents chance might put in his path on a given morning, with a regular daily rotation of names from the bottom of the list to the top. Come to think of it, I typed and retyped these names so often that I can recite for you numbers one through seven of his favored roster: numbers one through seven the important entries, since Brocklebank had determined that he was never likely to see more than seven cats out of his thirty at once.

He added: The magic number Young Rumrill had sought in order to best deceive the old man was stated clearly in the old man's notes, as I only discovered years later.

Brocklebank writes: This function of cat-fancying scarcely having been recognized; people being satisfied to use it and account for it simply as decorative, agreeable, unproblematic with respect to representation.

Rumrill said: The seven names were Trbuhovica, Obrh, Stržen, Rak, Pivka, Unica, and Ljubljanica. These were shortened in time to Trb, Ob, Strz, Rak, Piv, Un, and Ljub, respectively.

He added: The little imps.

Rumrill said: Note that Brocklebank did not personify or otherwise attribute familiar, comprehensible, anthropomorphic traits to his cats. Note that

I do not personify or otherwise attribute familiar et cetera traits to my own.

He added: Named or unnamed.

Rumrill said: It seemed to Brocklebank, and it seems now to me, that a cat, which is to say whatever unit of my household is possessed of those qualities that make such a designation possible, in polite company, without fear of contradiction or embarrassment—and which qualities I will not now enumerate, in case those attributes you yourself hold sacred as being indicative of such a unit's having earned the cognomen "cat" (whatever its *Vorname*, perhaps Scampers or Jean-Marie) bear little resemblance to my own, and that such a revelation might lead to discomfort or even repugnance on your parts as you restrain the urge to correct me or indeed retreat toward my front door, which you can only hope is still unlocked—it seemed to the old man, I say, and seems now to me, that each of our cats or "cats" is or was a machine designed not to comfort or complement the life of a solitary celibate, but for the manufacture of a particular condition or state or mode. Since I must and do take care of twenty cats and ten absences of cats, these latter unpresent only though force of will, it follows that *everything* I do and say and say to you or once upon a time to the grocer's boy is necessarily generated at least in part by this procedure.

He added: My daily routine, and by extension sensations, and by extension thoughts, and by extension existence.

Brocklebank writes: No cat-fancier working today must any longer assume that his next mode (of naming, of feeding) need remain in the same style, or inhabit the same world, as the one he's working on at the moment.

Rumrill said: I also think it unlikely that my cats personify or otherwise attribute personality traits to me, nor speculate as to my motives in the aftermath of this or that Rumrillian action. Surely, to them, I am no more than a convenient and happily discrete and self-sufficient system for the maintenance of their own habits, sensations, and thoughts: a clock-hand by whose revolutions they might count the days left to them before their respective feline expiries.

He added: And of course its own final tick.

Rumrill said: It is a kind of symbiosis: the maintenance of my cats acts to encourage and indeed enforce my own quotidian upkeep as a nominally healthy adult—male, I presume—which duty without being melodramatic has at times been something of a burden to me, since in my senescence and in the absence of records it has become more and more difficult to dispose of my time in what I could characterize as a constructive or agreeable manner. My cats, and the rigor of the series of actions and attitudes necessary for their maintenance, serve as a corrective to what we might call the gradual drift of my interest in—and the concurrent temptation to leave off the at-times tedious actions necessary to—my house and my self.

He added: Which is to say, Rumrill.

Rumrill said: I did not, for that matter, personify or otherwise attribute familiar, comprehensible, anthropomorphic personality traits to that sick, senile, old Austrian man, Mr. Brocklebank. I do not now, for that matter, personify or otherwise attribute any such personality traits to Mr. and Mrs. Pickles.

He added: In the interest of clarity.

Rumrill said: For that matter, I am fairly certain Mr. Brocklebank did not personify or attribute familiar et cetera traits to myself, in our "intimacy," as the time was not too far distant when his illness would progress to the point that he would have forgotten that he had ever forgotten that we didn't know each other very well. He wouldn't recognize me at all, that is; just as he couldn't tell his cats apart; but the beauty of his system was that recognition was irrelevant.

He added: Beauty, so to speak.

Brocklebank writes: My system lying between the two extremes of complete order and complete indeterminacy.

Rumrill said: Brocklebank had no interest in any single cat, which is to say a unit apprehended outside of the clockwork in concert with which this unit was meant to function. He was not, then, in this sense, an old man who owned thirty cats, since to him this thirty represented the minimum number to which his system might be reasonably applied.

He added: We might then as easily say, "Brocklebank was an old man with a cat."

Rumrill said: It would have been just as impossible for Brocklebank to identify this or that specific animal from his stock—say, were it to be abducted by persons unknown and then seen sitting in the window of another man's house—as it would be to explain the difference between the number 17 on the

marquee of a town bus and the number 17 on a cal-
endar. For Brocklebank, each unit of his menagerie
was equivalent to every other, no integer or note or
brick loved more or less than any of the others that
had been counted or struck or mortared to produce
his desired result.

He added: Otherwise, chaos.

Rumrill said: Brocklebank plotted their prospective courses through his home, and in his prime
would draw star charts mapping their orbits by day,
hour, month, minute: their circulation through
the I think the word is "rarefied" atmosphere of his
home. He even went so far as to graph their divaga-
tions on rice paper in numerous colors, so that their
manifold trajectories—influenced, if not instituted,
by Brocklebank himself, *primum movens*—could be
laid one atop the other and so overwrite the otherwise
insipid floor plan of his house (blueprints obtained
for a modest fee from our town-planning council):
unambitious parallelograms become prismatic laby-
rinths, baffling numina.

He added: The effortless complexity of an
obsessive.

Brocklebank writes: Noting that the freedom in
my system is not the freedom to be irresponsible.

Rumrill said: Each cat was only a digit in the
great and useless equation to which Brocklebank
devoted his widowerhood. Each cat was a bead on
the abacus that tallied the days of a life now empty
of any content or goal save its own enumeration:
Brocklebank's house a factory in which the hours of
the big world not ten yards distant from his patterned

rugs and gentle sconces could be denuded and refined till unfit for any application save the documentation of their own expenditure.

He added: And the foreman's efficiency.

Rumrill said: Not only did Brocklebank decline to give his cats permanent names, I don't think he often spoke to or even touched them. What mattered to the old man was his interaction with a closed system independent of, though still reliant upon, its genius loci.

He added: All eye and footstep.

Rumrill said: What mattered to the old man was the effect the care of his thirty cats would have upon his own perceptions, psyche, subject. In contrast to the big world beyond its walls, their little world—though no less indifferent, in its own way, to Brocklebank's experience of it—varied so much more dramatically day to day in its rhythms and tiny victories and the fall of light at this or that hour upon this or that whisker or gladiolus in perfect albeit arbitrary reaction to his performance as caretaker.

He added: Not to mention the gradual increase of his system's fatuous intricacy.

Rumrill said: As he told me, or tried to tell me, when I first took up my post, Trb for example could only take her water from a cylindrical vessel, while Ob only from a lentoid; Strz could drink from any vessel, but only while Piv or Un were on the ground floor; Rak could drink only from a vessel recently forsaken by Strz, but not if Piv or Un were still within one room of said vessel; Piv could drink only from a vessel then shared by Ob, but not if being watched by Llub. About Un, I fear, the less said the better.

He added: The Terrible Un.

Brocklebank writes: Difference having great importance, to be able to discriminate the difference in their pulse-rates, to know the smallest difference in their pulse-rates.

Rumrill said: "It is ideal," thought Brocklebank, I think, "if my regulations now require my presence at two or three locations in my home simultaneously. It is ideal," he went on to think, that endless putterer, that demon of increase, "if by increments the care of my household in its convolution fills my mind and occupies my sense of discipline and rewards my desire for symmetry, in these years of my decline, to the point at which the system of my cogency and the system of my household chores become a single glorious procedure that may continue to operate even after the inevitable breakdown of one or the other sympathetic collaborator."

He added: Due to fire, flood, famine.

Rumrill said: "By means of my procedure it may be possible to make from eye and hand and home, from mind and minded, a single unit," thought Brocklebank. "It little matters, should this stage be achieved, if a single element, apprehended individually, be removed by chance or design from the harmonious totality."

He added: "No more," continued Brocklebank, "than the loss of a single cell out of millions might trouble even the most diligent and conscientious nervous system."

Rumrill said: "Would that I could preside over a greater parcel of the big world, and bring my system to bear upon its inhabitants. Would that the elements of my composition could themselves be as complex, potentially, as a Brocklebank."

He added: Oh, ambitious senescence!

Brocklebank writes: Noting that the results of my system are subtle, often too much so for the average cat-fancier to discern, I nonetheless accept this obstacle to the comprehension of my works.

Rumrill said: Brocklebank thought, "A post office, a train station, a town or city or state would in their greater ramification better suit my ends. I can only imagine in my malodorous feebleness the harmony that might be made by millions of men and women in melodious mutuality to manufacture in their daily dither a single process, a single machinery that would struggle and succeed despite the fragility and imperfection of its components to rise to a collective self-regard and begin a new and relentless perception of itself and the big world made small at last by its encompassment within the system of Brocklebank."

He added: With carbon copies on pink onionskin.

Rumrill said: "My millennium," the old man went on, sadly, I suppose, "can only occur here, in miniature, in the little space that I am still able to subject to my own ineffectual preferences. I may however continue to hope that even on the scale of a rank and colorblind widower and his thirty near-feral cats, I might make an edifice worthy of some admiration, might make a mind from the many simple processes in my care—no mind can ever be more than the sum of its processes—and so participate in something imperishable, something more durable than the flawed and haunted Austrian imprisoned here in his habits, tastes, and hatreds, unwound in rusty malfunction."

He added: (Too much?)

Rumrill said: Brocklebank thought, "Thus would I become insensible to the discomforts of this quotidian Brocklebank, because no longer simply an untidy primate but myself the principle behind a small and orderly system within the large and vulgar system or systems that compose the big world and its indifference to anything that cannot de- or replace the assumptions that govern it. Though my tools be undignified, I intend nonetheless to plow my furrow until I burrow straight through to the center of the earth."

He added: Or something.

Brocklebank writes: Some of these attitudes, ungenerous or radical, generous or conservative, toward institutions dear to many, no doubt giving impressions unfavorable to my thought and personality.

Rumrill said: A truly new medium leads to the development of impressions that can only be expressed by means of that medium. One can only communicate by means of Brocklebank's system those things Brocklebank's system might teach us to express.

He added: And we've learned.

Brocklebank writes: My contribution to this publication seeking not to pose a problem in the hope that someone else has already found a solution and is prepared to let me know about it; nor to present a solution to a problem which other people might be tackling at the moment.

Rumrill said: The first time this great pioneer refused to

step outside, he stopped a Brocklebank-sized pace from the open air and told me, "It's too cold for me to go out. I'm not dressed warm."

He added: "Mr. Brocklebank," I replied, "this ain't out."

Rumrill said: "This ain't out," I told him. "And in any case, it ain't cold."

He added: And it wasn't.

Rumrill said: Brocklebank then told me that his shoe had split, the left. Brocklebank was worried water might get into it, though no rain was forecast that day, and there had been no rain recently, nor in recent memory.

He added: It had probably never rained in our town.

Rumrill said: Brocklebank assumed that the likelihood of its beginning to rain beyond his door was somehow increased by there being a point of access in his shoe, the left, for any water that might fall and collect along his sovereign thoroughfares. Brocklebank was of the opinion that the likelihood of its *having already rained* was increased by there being a point of access in his et cetera.

He added: Such were the verities of the cosmos inhabited by Brocklebank in his decline.

Rumrill said: A quality shared by youth, old age, and individuals of whatever span who have experienced extended isolation is the inability to distinguish interior and exterior states. So I offered to put some electrician's tape over the hole in Brocklebank's shoe.

He added: A bluff.

Rumrill said: Brocklebank eventually resorted to the statement that he was too tired for his constitutional. I wasn't sure whether he meant to imply that our conversation itself had tired him, or whether this tiredness had been the root cause for his previous, hoax excuses.

He added: Put succinctly.

Rumrill said: Once Brocklebank had exhausted all the forms of weather that could have served as a rationale for his inertia, or rather as rationales he thought would be sufficient to convince his assistant to abandon his determination to force his employer out the front door, Brocklebank resorted to the tack that he was too tired to run any errands on that day in any case. I couldn't be certain whether this was a barb intended to make me feel guilty for my good-natured opposition to his project (to stay put) from the moment he'd proposed it in opposition to my own project (his daily constitutional), or whether this tiredness was the root cause for his earlier, sham excuses, which he hadn't, for reasons of pride (or what served as pride in the absence of any proudness), wanted to admit, however long ago, at the beginning of our exhausting colloquy, even though this might well have forestalled what had now become a tiresome bit of repartee for the both of us.

He added: With carbon copies on pink onionskin.

Rumrill said: A third explanation for Brocklebank's final sally on the subject of his refusal to take a walk would be that he had seized on the excuse of tiredness secure in the knowledge that this would be the one alibi I would have no way to gain-say. Someone of Brocklebank's plausible age cannot be told that they aren't really tired.

He added: Try it and see.

Rumrill said: Need I add that the tiredness of Brocklebank was necessarily an abstraction to Rumrill? The tiredness of Brocklebank had no more substance than a radio report on a solar flare or foreign epidemic or missile en route over the sea.

He added: As the tiredness of Rumrill, or indeed the word "radio," are necessarily abstractions to you.

Brocklebank writes: Now evolving a whole symbolic world, perceiving myself as in a wormlike state, totally diminished from humanity.

Rumrill said: The woman in the stacks, long gone by the time Brocklebank first refused to leave his house, long since carried away by the estimable blue and red diesel-fed Express train to the city nearest our town—a line that was discontinued soon after; or did she in fact take the last of the outbound runs?—was my superior when I was first hired at the library. When the woman in the stacks resigned her position at the library to travel far, I assume, from any Rumrill, her own superior wasn't for a moment discomfited by the suspicion that I, given my seniority, ought to be considered for promotion, to fill her now vacant position.

He added: As somewhere in the world my erstwhile "friend" woke early and unhappy, another day older, in the din of the shrill, amplified muezzin's call through her glassless window.

Rumrill said: I admit I was less than dutiful in my work at the library. I had become aware some time before that there were no consequences for dereliction.

He added: Nor, apparently, rewards for distinction.

Rumrill said: I spent as much work time as

possible in the corridors of the library, on my way to or from the restrooms. I drank as much water as possible so as to necessitate many trips away from whatever tasks the woman in the stacks, or her eventual replacement, had assigned.

He added: Happiest in those long and narrow corridors.

Rumrill said: The library's layout led me to deduce that the building had not been intended for use as a library when it was first built. It seemed to me that, for example, whoever had designed the building had done so with the intention that it be easily defended.

He added: From whom I could not say.

Rumrill said: The library's layout was such that when you left one room to go to another—to use the restroom, or else squirt a little cold water from the adjacent water fountains on a stain before it could set—and another person was headed in the opposite direction—to the innermost stacks to consult a book, for example, on the Hagia Sophia—both perambulators would be forced to face one another for considerably longer than any two strangers, or even any two more or less friendly acquaintances, are ever under ordinary circumstances subjected to each others' direct scrutiny. There was also the sound of their footsteps on the tile, which could be heard long enough in advance for the rhythm of it to create an unbearable suspense.

He added: Mostly, we kept our eyes down.

Rumrill said: Surely my own eventual resignation made the library a less substantial place for my coworkers. Surely it was an impoverishment of their daily lives that I could no longer be relied upon to sit at my desk in observation of them at all hours of the day, that I could no longer be relied upon to substantiate them, to confirm them in their opinions of themselves as livers of life superior to poor maladroit Rumrill—the thin gruel of their own observations as undisturbed by novelty in my absence as the section of the stacks consecrated to Byzantine architecture.

He added: Wholly unfrequented.

Rumrill said: I wish that I had kept a diary or journal or perhaps a series of typed notes as thick as a book to help me tell you, now, and through you who knows what others, what exactly were the motives of the woman in the stacks when she decided to leave the library and library vis-à-vis Rumrill. Unfortunately, all I would have kept or typed at the time were those pages for Mr. Brocklebank.

He added: With carbon copies on pink onionskin.

Rumrill said: You could say that Mr. Brocklebank replaced the woman in the stacks, insofar as they were the foci of my life at different stages in my evolution. You could say that the former and the latter were each my significant others.

He added: Though with othernesses of variable significance.

Rumrill said: From a mostly absent man who had paid me to feed his cats and ensure that no one vandalized or burglarized his home in his absence, Brocklebank had become a real and burdensome presence. I might have resented him for this reformation, though naturally I was free to resign from his service at any time.

He added: As from the library.

Rumrill said: When Brocklebank proposed that I become his secretary as well as cat-sitter, I remember that my initial assignment was to type and then collate, assemble, and bind those pages, those same unfeasible instructions for the maintenance of thirty nameless cats as I had been handed when I arrived for my initial interview with the old man. I can't account for the obvious discrepancy in this: since Young Rumrill was handed just such a typescript, already typed and collated and assembled and bound, on the aforementioned occasion when he was first entrusted with Brocklebank's cats, how could it have been my job to type and collate and assemble and bind the self-same document?

He added: Consternation.

Brocklebank writes: Cat-fancying being the negation of any actually accessible lived experience.

Rumrill said: I wish that I had kept a diary or series of typed notes as thick as a book to record, for my convenience, the details of the scene of the farewell between the woman in the stacks and myself. I could then consult these notes and give you a summary as to the disposition of this event both physically and temporally, which would allow you to imagine the scene with some degree of exactitude.

He added: Probably it was in the stacks.

Brocklebank writes: Substance having nothing to do with character.

Rumrill said: It didn't escape my coworkers'

notice, when I tendered my resignation, that I'd advanced from the care of Brocklebank's cats to the care of Brocklebank *and* his cats. They asked if this, at least, could be considered a promotion.

He added: My first.

Rumrill said: In the pedestrian tunnel to the electric train, on my last day at the library, on my way home, which would take me as usual over our town's only bridge—barely the height of a church steeple, but which long-time residents still refer to as the "Shrieking Bridge," given that for years it was the only edifice hereabouts from which anyone could conceivably have thrown themselves in the hopes of an injury greater than a mild sprain—a teenage boy, with three other teenage boys, poked me, almost punched me, in my left shoulder, as they walked at me from the other end of the tunnel, which is to say toward the library instead of away from it. The boy admonished me, as I assume he had in the past been admonished, and perhaps by someone looking not unlike me, *don't run*.

He added: A misinterpretation of my majestic stride.

Rumrill said: I began to carry a knife after this episode, when I went out, perhaps to sit at an outdoor café, or to purchase something on Brocklebank's behalf. I would hold the knife's very small rubber handle in my right hand, hidden in my right-hand pocket, in anticipation of a second encounter with the boy.

He added: Which seemed inevitable.

Rumrill said: If I was to encounter his little horde again, and he moved toward me with aggressive intent—or moved toward me at all—I would take the knife out of my pocket. I would stand on one of the boy's feet and take him by the hair at the back of his head.

He added: Not without luster.

Rumrill said: I would move the knife upward into his neck and jaw from underneath, and words like "tide" and "gristle" and "burble" would cross my mind as the small sharp edge parted skin and vein and tongue and palate in a determined arc whose intended endpoint was no less exalted a locale than the young master's septum. His head would be unable to work itself free from my grip, even with its arsenal of shrieks and spasms, and his friends of course would be too surprised and then disgusted to set foot into the immediate area of my torrential intervention.

He added: Which torrent would be a balm to the dry skin on my nose.

Rumrill said: The knife would be lost, and Rumrill's hand also mangled in the execution of his surgical revenge. The boy, on the ground, would give out with some last mangled blurts whose origins deep within his basal ganglia might perhaps constitute a message from the swamps of prehistory as to the uselessness of all Mammalian endeavor.

He added: *Allas, departynge of our compaignye!*

Rumrill said: It was on some Brocklebankian errand, my thoughts occupied by just such a rehearsal of my triumph, that I did indeed run into the boys a second time. I was shouldered off of the sidewalk and onto the street; surprised, I stumbled and landed on one knee, which was torn—skin and fabric—by some gravel.

He added: Not even especially sharp.

Rumrill said: They deigned to notice me when I gave evidence of my pain with one or two shrewd squeaks (for the encounter had till this point retained the character of an accident, not worth an interruption in their conversation about, I think, dodecaphony). Turning all of their six or eight eyes on me, they called out a litany of nouns intended in all kindness to euthanize what remained of my dignity.

He added: "Clochard, collion, gowk, kike, jobbernowl, harrow, pautonnier . . ."

Brocklebank writes: The revolution we were making being not then or now appreciated.

Rumrill said: Perhaps I have mentioned that Brocklebank toward the end of his life could not rely on his memory. By "rely" I mean "make practical use of."

He added: And by "make practical use of," I mean "rely."

Rumrill said: I have said that this loss of memory began "toward the end of his life," but I don't know how long Brocklebank's deterioration had developed before we first met. It seemed that the procedures he had developed to organize his days—centered around the maintenance of his thirty cats, and in his so-called spare time the elaboration of this same system via a series of typed notes and eventually dictation to yours truly—had all been constructed, by design or accident, to function without interruption even should the memory of their originator fail.

He added: So long as certain postulates remained undisturbed.

Rumrill said: Bad as Brocklebank's memory became, some details, older details, were inviolate, and could not be touched by the blight. These became, as I imagined it, outposts from which Brocklebank was able to make sallies into a landscape otherwise featureless, variable, unpredictable.

He added: Desert.

Rumrill said: Away from these solid certainties, I would observe him with no little fascination as he was forced to make and then make again basic deductions about those parts of his life that persisted, on a daily basis, in his attention. What persisted, day to day, were the material circumstances of his house, person, and helpmeet.

He added: Which is to say, Rumrill.

Rumrill said: I watched as, in the absence of information, Brocklebank's behavior modulated away from what we might call sincerity—defined here as the knowledge arrived at without deliberation of how he should react to the stimuli the world had placed before him—to a subjunctive mode, in that he was forced to make do with guesses. I can tell you that his guesses were, given his condition, remarkable.

He added: Exercises in the creative utilization of the combinatorial potential of those objects and their attributes now arranged by his life-to-date for his senescent apprehension.

Rumrill said: I could cite the presence of those photographs of his sterile and now subterranean wife still on display at that time in Brocklebank's bedroom and living room—in the latter case a wedding picture in gaudy plastic frame that depicted husband and wife in casual dress (because, I assumed, of the war), she with a handful of flowers or flowering weeds that look, even given the cheap film, the lack of color, the smudges and fingerprints on the glass over the print, and of course its great age, entirely pitiful—and the less said about her hat, which I hope was borrowed, the better. These launched the old man regularly into a series of deductions that only at great intervals landed within any proximity to the probability that this woman could have been, once, *the* or *a* Mrs. Brocklebank—though I noted that the old man could always identify himself, in whatever picture, as a young man.

He added: Conveniently enough.

Rumrill said: I remember Brocklebank's theory that the photograph was of someone else's wedding, and that he had been present at the occasion only to congratulate the new bride. A variant was that the picture was indeed from his own wedding, but that the woman in question was only a friend of the actual bride, Brocklebank's wife-to-be, who was somewhere off frame when the photo was taken, amused to allow her very best girlfriend to pose in poignant mock anticipation of her own special day, which of course never came, since she died not long after.

He added: Because of the war, I assumed.

Rumrill said: I remember Brocklebank's theory that the woman in the picture, which had again been deemed entirely fraudulent, needed to have such a photograph taken for legal reasons, for example to get a visa from whatever government had first granted Brocklebank asylum. Brocklebank had no trouble with the idea that he as a young man would have been so charitable and chivalrous as to help the poor woman and arrange this sham-wedding snapshot.

He added: And no trouble with the idea that as an old man he would have so keen a sense of fun as to hang this hoax memento in his home as though it were legitimate.

Rumrill said: I remember Brocklebank's theory that the picture, which did indeed have a "join" or crease down its middle, probably from being folded in two, shoved in the pocket of a jacket on his passage overseas, was the product of some darkroom legerdemain, and that the groom, which is to say Brocklebank, on the left side of the picture, whose eyes were on his lapel, perhaps worried some specks of dandruff had flaked onto an otherwise unsuspicious shirtfront, had no notion that he'd been wedded by artful forgers (green visors over their squinty eyes) to this cheery young lady for purposes unknown. Purposes such as, for example, a plot to sell his poor old bachelor's house away from him while he was away on one of his supposed trips abroad: an older woman who resembled or perhaps was in fact the young lady from the photograph, though now half a century older, would pop up to pose again as his wife and sign the appropriate papers for a considerable emolument.

He added: Said appropriate papers now in the hands of developers desperate to put up more of those cramped and damp apartment blocks you young and unhappy husbands and wives now, in your turn, inhabit.

Rumrill said: I remember Brocklebank's theory that, alternatively, a cabal of neighbors might have produced the forged photograph in order to imply the existence of a family member who could, given Brocklebank's infirmity, make the appropriate legal arrangements to have the old man put in a rest home. The neighbors hated the smell of his house, the look of it, with its jovial lawn torn up in favor of gray and easily tended gravel; the smell of Brocklebank and the look of him, a klaxon to the eye, a one-man harlequinade; the smell of his cats and the look of them as they stared in the manner of cats out the nineteen windows of his plausible house at the neighbors' own progress toward a similar infirmity; Brocklebank's life, his life's work, filed in nineteen drawers divided between three steel filing cabinets, meaning six point three three repeating each, full from first inch to last of his typed notes, his opus, his system.

He added: Which, too, smelled.

Rumrill said: I remember Brocklebank's theory—the acme of his senile lucubration—that our town was no longer a proper town at all, but a community closed off in order to quarantine its occupants from the general population of the nation while we condemned men and women awaited eventual liquidation in said nation's great ovens: inmates who were for reasons ideological, sanitary, racial, or judicial (or ideo-sanitary, racio-judiciary, et cetera) an unacceptable influence on the innocent citizens who were still suffered to wander free beyond our poorly patrolled border, and fit now for no fate but the bakery. Hence, he said, our *volunteer* fire department, less interested in the rescue of property or people than in liquor and arguments about epistemology; hence, he said, the *deterioration* of our civic infrastructure, poisoned not so much by incompetence as by the lassitude of unsupervised prison trustees, in line for eventual execution and so with no incentive to prolong the farce.

He added: Why, after all, bother?

Rumrill said: Hence, he added, the gangs of nearly feral children born here in captivity and so very eager for any sensation as to steal Brocklebank's medications; hence the vagrants who prowled the streets and liked to play at organized resistance but who were in the end nothing more than *naughty schoolboys* who passed silly notes and smelled of piss. Hence the endless supply of stray or discarded housecats, their owners or keepers vanished or summarily disposed of; hence the disappearance of his dear wife under mysterious circumstances, and the installation into his home of a *kapo* paid to pose as an amanuensis and sabotage Brocklebank's vital work, ordered to ensure that nothing provocative, nothing that might undermine the status quo, ever be transmitted to the great world beyond our township.

He added: How perspicacious.

Brocklebank writes: There being a time when I thought that perhaps I could gain some kind of appropriate position among intellectuals in other fields by appealing not to their capacity to discern the soundness of my system but by the sense of my words.

Rumrill said: It was around this point, perhaps

even in the middle of that same conversation, or one that was no different, that a bill collector came to call. He knocked at Brockebank's door and said he had come to collect the rent.

He added: With a tie and no mustache.

Rumrill said: I told his tie that the rent had been paid; in fact, there was no rent to pay because Brocklebank owned his home; in fact, he had the wrong house, and since I signed Brocklebank's checks for him, I could even provide evidence of these assertions—a novel sensation. Still, the bill collector insisted that the old man was several months in arrears.

He added: Consternation.

Rumrill said: Brocklebank invited the interloper into his house, in my despite. In my despite, Brocklebank offered his chair, a very combustible overstuffed number in which I had never been allowed to sit, and offered the man refreshment too, served with his own hands, which though they trembled managed nonetheless to deliver the majority of their payload to the intended recipient.

He added: Who was no doubt unaccustomed to such kindness.

Rumrill said: It transpired that the rent in question was due not for the house in which we three held our pleasant colloquy, but for an apartment in our town center, not far from the public library. It transpired that Brocklebank had rented it some years before.

He added: And that it showed evidence of regular if spartan habitation.

Rumrill said: Something had changed in the meantime, for now the rooms stood unaired and abandoned. At last the managers had stirred from their torpor, after who knows how many months, in order to take action against delinquent Brocklebank by way of this smiler and his tie and his shoes.

He added: Or take action against Brocklebank's estate, if he'd died.

Rumrill said: It was two damp rooms with bath. There was a bed and a few distressed travel posters, said the bill collector, and a backlog of what must have been several annums' worth of mail.

He added: From various defunct consulates.

Rumrill said: The bill collector was of the opinion that the old man had once kept a mistress in the apartment, or a series of mistresses, who had perhaps tired of Brocklebank, or vice versa; or perhaps he simply couldn't get it up any longer—it happens. Brocklebank was unoffended by this suggestion, or did not understand it.

He added: Or maybe there was an illegitimate child, or children?

Rumrill said: I nursed certain suspicions as to what purpose the apartment had really served. Though I had no intention of satisfying the bill collector's curiosity.

He added: Or anyone else's.

Rumrill said: Brocklebank naturally had no memory of the apartment. Brocklebank naturally had no memory of the use or uses to which he had once put it.

He added: And rather favored the mistress hypothesis, I could tell.

Rumrill said: To put an end to this nauseating

episode, as I watched the bill collector pour what I supposed to be iced tea down into his throat, I asked the man or his clothes to convey to his employers that Brocklebank would no longer need the apartment, and that they might as well rent it to whatever young couple would be so foolish as to find its precincts adequate for their new lives as residents of our town. I was tickled, I confess, as I gave these instructions, not only by the unquestioned puissance I had demonstrated over the old man's affairs, but by the thought that whomever came to occupy the apartment would never suspect that it had at one time been the sovereign soil, so to speak, of a foreign country.

He added: An embassy of the great empire of mendacity.

Brocklebank writes: The user hardly exerting any influence on this system, he cannot express any particular wishes, he can only decide whether to accept the results or to reject them if he does not want to try to steer the data toward the lines of his own understanding by interpreting it very freely.

Rumrill said: The old man only got worse, after we had disposed of the bill collector. I don't mean by this that Brocklebank forgot more and more of the things that had happened to him in his preposterous life before Rumrill, nor even that he forgot the few things that continued to happen to him in his preposterous life *with* Rumrill, but that memory as a function of Brocklebank the animal, in its final agonies, came to be crowded out entirely by the related but I think substantially dissimilar function we call habit.

He added: Do you understand the difference?

Brocklebank writes: An openness to the totality of interactions implying a tendency away from traditional structures, toward informality.

Rumrill said: Brocklebank toward the end of his life was unable to identify me at all. My name or the names of the actions I had performed the previous feeble day or hour were to Brocklebank's mind no more accessible than the contents of an unread book on ancient architecture.

He added: *The Aesthetic Purpose of Byzantine and Roman Colonnades, with Divers Other Essays*, by C. de Secondat Rumrill.

Rumrill said: Still, though I had become as inexplicable to him as that photo of his late wife, he no more questioned the appropriateness of my presence in his household than he had questioned my suitability to occupy this position to begin with, the very first time I reported for duty at his house to take indifferent if not wholly negligent care of his thirty cats, and, eventually, with an analogous degree of probity, take care of the man himself. We might say that nothing much changed over the many years we spent together, since—first day or last—Brocklebank never once recognized me.

He added: Not, anyway, as Rumrill.

Rumrill said: As regarded my duties, since Brocklebank often couldn't remember what he'd already instructed me to do, and couldn't remember what still needed to be done, my work for him came to seem a perpetual present tense, in which no errand could be run and no chore completed to the old man's satisfaction. Either the motive for his initial request would evaporate at some moment prior to my completion of the chore I'd been instructed to undertake, or else the request would be retained in Brocklebank's memory but the actions necessary to its fulfillment come to seem, to his eyes, unrelated.

He added: And when I took dictation, he would repeat the same words or sentences until his mouth was too dry to squeak.

Rumrill said: Often I returned with his groceries only to be met with a ravel of incredulous invective. How much did I think he could eat, he demanded; didn't the pantry already groan with all the offal I'd picked out for him the last time; his last dinars spent only to fill his house with food that would spoil on the shelves.

He added: When the cupboards were in fact bare.

Rumrill said: I often returned with his groceries only to find him huddled in the corner, because this is where one huddles: he'd assumed I had abandoned him, he'd been alone so long. How cruel I'd been to stay away, he wept; not even to call; to leave him to fend for himself, when I knew how ill he'd been; I was a disappointment, a monster; there was no excuse for it; what a curse he was too weak now to find someone else to help him, whoever I was.

He added: When it had been he who'd called me and insisted I buy this or that.

Brocklebank writes: Governing this tendency—reining it in—are various thoroughly traditional pet-care structures such as grooming, play, regular feeding times, *usw.*, in each of which reposes a portion of the history of cat-fancying.

Rumrill said: I feel obliged to admit that I was

also less than dutiful where it came to Brocklebank's dictation, even at the beginning. I feel obliged to admit that I transcribed only enough to convince him that I had kept pace.

He added: Enough sometimes if he could hear the typewriter clatter.

Rumrill said: I also didn't bother to keep his notes in order. I filed them away in whichever drawer was most convenient at the time.

He added: Preferably one already open.

Rumrill said: The dutiful execution of my tasks, both as nurse and angel of record, was irrelevant. I mean irrelevant not just to myself, but also to Brocklebank.

He added: Unbeknownst to him.

Rumrill said: Brocklebank made many demands, but was unable now to see or understand how those demands might be addressed or improved by direct action. The knowledge that I was engaged in the supposed satisfaction of his demands was as close as he could get to said satisfaction.

He added: Even if I did my damnedest.

Rumrill said: Brocklebank had become a more or less autonomous system for the generation of demands. But these demands could not and did not need to be met.

He added: Widower Brocklebank a system that operated irrespective of causality.

Rumrill said: Often I typed whatever I pleased, all day, as he recited; one hour much the same as the next, from the time of my arrival until my departure—on those nights, I mean, when I was allowed to go home. Often I started off dutifully but then lapsed into the transcription of whatever nonsense crossed my mind, in preference to what came out of Brocklebank's mouth.

He added: Gobbledygook in either case.

Rumrill said: Often, after a poor start, I would feel guilty; I would feel that I had made a mockery of the old man's inability to collate the many moments of his day or life. By the time it was dark, I would again be hard at it, obediently, and with no thought for my own comfort.

He added: Which was, indeed, significantly abridged.

Rumrill said: Soon enough, however, I again recalled that Brocklebank had brought me into his employ under false pretenses. Soon enough I remembered the bill collector, and the mysterious apartment, and the likelihood that all of Brocklebank's stories were probably as groundless as my conviction that I might one day see again the woman in the stacks.

He added: Unless she too was only holed up in some squalid rental downtown.

Rumrill said: Soon enough I would again want to punish the old man for his intention to trap me, for reasons unknown—a trap in which I had allowed myself to be caught, for reasons not much clearer. Then, just as soon, I would be reminded that you can't really punish an animal without memory.

He added: Any more than an animal without a memory can lie.

Rumrill said: If Brocklebank had deceived me intentionally, those stories he had told of his world travels, back when I was employed at the public library, had no more substance now than any of his earnest if incorrect explanations for the disposition of the objects in his home. If there was any difference now for Brocklebank between a deliberate untruth and an erroneous theorem, he could not see it.

He added: And so neither could I.

Rumrill said: Similarly, I couldn't say if there was any qualitative difference between the prose I produced for the old man when I typed simply to allow him to hear the typewriter clack and ding, and then the prose I put out when Brocklebank had (nearly) my complete attention. For example, I remember—though I can no longer find the page in my archives—the statement "Cats hatch faster in stone."

He added: Among other, little-known trivia.

Rumrill said: As a result of my disinclination to transcribe every word spoken by Brocklebank during this terminal phase of what I might term our business relationship, one could make the case that I acted inappropriately, that whatever the sinister or senile Austrian had or had not done to me, my actions were a deliberate betrayal of an invalid's confidence. One could, indeed, make the case that I maliciously sabotaged the completion of what a helpless crank thought of as his great contribution to an admittedly obscure and inconsequential discipline, and which he hoped would in some obscure way assure his immortality.

He added: Or, better said, *persistence in the world*.

Rumrill said: I might defend myself with the argument that Brocklebank's illness, if it was an illness, was the real saboteur, and not my itinerant attentions. I regret to say, however, that I never paid the business enough mind to know for certain whether or not Brocklebank's statements might have accumulated in time—had a better Rumrill attended him—to become a work of, who knows, genius.

He added: Or something.

Rumrill said: I felt, no doubt out of self-interest and laziness—the twin stars by which I navigate this life—that my chief duty then was to keep Brocklebank convinced that his work was forever "in progress." Progress was all he could understand.

He added: Eternal progress toward no goal.

Rumrill said: I wish that I could say that my poor performance as the old man's aide was motivated by pettiness, by a desire to repay my employer for his many cruelties, be they miniature or Machiavellian. When I said my good mornings or good nights to Mr. Brocklebank, I could never be certain whether I shook the hand of a shrewd persecutor or a pitiable automaton.

He added: In either case, soon to wind down forever.

Rumrill said: He had a temper, even then; he would I'm sure have tormented the children he never produced, if he had produced them, and who in their nonexistence should count themselves lucky to have escaped manifestation as whelps of *Familie* Brocklebank. He even tried, on some days, to hurt me, physically, to reprimand me for my behavior, or rather his interpretation of my behavior.

He added: Flawed.

Brocklebank writes: One hardly needing to seek out personality, as it can never be avoided.

Rumrill said: He took my wrist in his hand one evening as it and I made progress by majestic lengths past his apparent repose in a chaise longue. He had propped himself in the semi-circle of warmth generated by his fireplace, or rather the fire in his fireplace; this is how the scene suggests itself to me, or would do.

He added: If he'd had a fireplace.

Rumrill said: He held onto my wrist and wrenched my hand and arm out of their accustomed orbits, frustrating the nonchalant and wholly symmetrical pendulum of my progress past his station and into the tiny fruit-fly filled kitchen. I was yanked to a standstill and embarrassed at my shriek.

He added: Ambushed!

Rumrill said: What perplexed me, or perplexed me most, was the absence of apparent motive, the absence of threat—the absence of Brocklebank's attention, even, to the betrayal, if not to say workplace abuse, just effected by his left hand and arm. Both of his eyes remained pointed at his newspaper.

He added: Head canted in disinterested declination.

Rumrill said: The next perplexity in line was that which I felt at my inability despite the old man's reputed frailty to disengage myself from his grip. He held me there until I gave a second squeal and kicked his chair, which then tipped for a moment of disequilibrium toward the fire that did not roar a few paces distant.

He added: Upon which reversal his two Austrian

eyes, pristine of ill intention, rose at last from their *Zeitung*.

Rumrill said: What perplexed Brocklebank, when he deigned to look at me—red welts in the shape of his fingers squeezed into my outraged meat—was his employee possessed now of the conviction that nothing less than bloody murder could possibly wash away this slight: murder perhaps with knives, perhaps with fire, no, nothing less would let me feel that he had been repaid. Whereas the next perplexity in line for Rumrill was the sight of my employer with all of his malice toward reason and mankind—which had been made naked for a moment's time on no discernable pretense—again clothed in the shabby, innocuous dress to which, all these years unsuspected, it had been confined.

He added: And nary a crease out of place.

Rumrill said: At other times, there was almost an amity between us. We, two bachelors, or rather one widower and one bachelor, in any case two celibates by necessity, both concentrated upon our work, or rather Brocklebank's work, which he had managed to make mine as well, with perhaps present in each of our minds the unpresent woman who had not seen fit to remain in our companies.

He added: And so rescue us from one another.

Rumrill said: Soon after the arm incident I dumped all of Brocklebank's German-language books off the Shrieking Bridge, down into our town's famous railway graveyard—the books for which he had abandoned so many other possessions, in order to make room in his one suitcase on his way to this country; which suitcase, by the way, went down with them, to become a bird's nest, perhaps, or a badger's lair. The bindings of the books were so weak from so many years so wet in our town that I saw loose pages flutter or sail through the doorframe of an upended passenger car, to be perused there by who knows what uncomprehending eyes until it and they returned to dust.

He added: The approved way to dispose of garbage in our town.

Brocklebank writes: Some people not thinking it's so witty, but I suppose everybody has a different sense of humor, and not everybody can enjoy the same kinds of things.

Rumrill said: The evening after the evening on which he injured my arm I returned to my apartment after the usual pantomime of Brocklebank's dictation to overhear a news item of some interest being discussed by my neighbors on their balcony. It's unlikely that I was meant to be included in their conversation.

He added: But likely I listened nevertheless.

Rumrill said: This anecdote had occurred, in its first instance—I mean, before it was an anecdote—in our own neighborhood. Our daily mail was then delivered by a man driving a white van.

He added: Strange to say.

Rumrill said: One of the men in one of the white vans was unable, one morning, for this or that reason—indigestion, perhaps; or a hangnail; or confusion as to the distinction between the phenomenal and noumenal worlds—to complete his rounds. Whatever the cause, this man drove home at the end of his workday with his white van still full of the pieces of mail he ought to have delivered.

He added: We might spend a moment in contemplation of a white van's worth of thwarted correspondence.

Rumrill said: The next morning, the man could not but admit to himself that his previous day's malfeasance was already, as they say, more than his job was worth. He was soon provided with another whole day's worth of mail to be delivered, however, which delivery would necessarily take an entire day's worth of time—and this in addition to the necessity that he dispose of the full day's worth of mail he had hoarded, for whatever reason, in the previous cycle.

He added: Consternation.

Rumrill said: The man put his next allotment of mail in the back of his white van and drove around our town in goalless circuit, unable to think of a solution. The man in his white van must have told himself that there was still a chance he could "catch up" afterhours, or on Sunday, or in any case "on the side," so that his failures would not be discovered.

He added: And yet, already a certain lassitude.

Rumrill said: On the next day this man once again reported for work and picked up his next day's allotment of mail. He once again drove around our town in his white van, with three days' worth of anxiety, and three days' worth of our letters, on board.

He added: To make not a single delivery.

Rumrill said: You see, to deliver even a single letter would make the weight of all the undelivered letters unbearable. To deliver even a single letter would be to admit that a restoration of his previous way of life was impossible.

He added: Would be to crash back to earth from the state of weightless, enviable virtuality he had, without forethought, attained.

Rumrill said: The town, and by extension the big world beyond the town, and by extension the little world of our town's post office, its procedures and expectations, all still appeared to function despite what the man would previously have assumed to be an impossible, unacceptable breakdown in its processes. He had trespassed upon the foundational assumptions around which his life, and the lives of his colleagues, and by extension the lives of his fellow human beings, had been organized.

He added: Yet the trump of doom had not sounded.

Rumrill said: To upset this providential balance between catastrophe and routine, to make any attempt at redress or confession, would be to invite who knew what horrors, and, more to the point, common unhappiness back into his life, back into the world. Whereas once he had worried about such things as being late, or about delivering such-and-such a parcel to the wrong address, or perhaps about that new pain which had developed in his lower back, or perhaps about those compromising letters written by his wife or significant other that he had recently discovered, by chance, behind a green radiator, *now* he could not manage to worry even about mortality, or the eventual collapse of our town and the big world upon which it was founded into our welcoming sun.

He added: All deliveries, large and small, suspended.

Rumrill said: Our man had become an astronaut. What a surprise it was to him to find how easy it was, how little it had taken—no more, indeed, than a moment's inattention—to float away and find himself too far from solid ground to work his way back.

He added: Such was his velocity.

Rumrill said: The days and weeks piled up, as did the sacks of undelivered mail, and still no one punished, dismissed, or even upbraided our delinquent. He could hardly ask any of his colleagues, much less his superiors, why no notice had been paid to his transgressions.

He added: Too great a risk not only of reprimand, but of confirmation that the man had after all ceased to exist.

Rumrill said: I don't know how much time passed between his initial lapsus and the climax, so called, of the anecdote. We should insert here an ellipsis of no less than a month, but not so long as to strain your credulity.

He added: Ladies' choice.

Rumrill said: The man came to feel that he had received a dispensation, the fabled opportunity to visit one's own funeral, to see how the world would get along without him. He watched his coworkers, his neighbors, his sexual partner or partners, his animals and bedclothes and coffee grounds all continue their perambulations down their respective thoroughfares, all without comment, without criticism, without the least notice paid to his departure from the bounds of acceptable behavior: he, the thrilling or astonishing spaceman, unmoored, past rescue; he, the ghost who walks and leaves no footprint.

He added: A very practical afterlife.

Rumrill said: The man could not help but wonder, as would I, as would even a Pickle, surely, what else he might be able to get away with. So long as he accepted that nothing he did or said (or refused to do, or forgot to do) would ever have an appreciable result, would ever raise comment—so long, I mean, as he could make peace with the knowledge that no obscenity he could commit would ever discommode the world or its inhabitants—was it not the case that he could kill, eat, rape, burn, mangle, micturate upon whomever, whatever, whichever?

He added: Without fear of reprisal?

Rumrill said: Was it not true that, with a van full of dead letters as ballast for his quotidian worries, the man was free to aspire to thoughts and actions of which he could not previously have dreamed? Was it not true that he had become nothing less than a postal deity, powerless to effect even the smallest change, I grant you, yet omnipotent too, in his way, with the entirety of the world for his playground—free to roam though zones of irrelevance undreamed of by his colleagues in their respective, regularly emptied vans?

He added: The undisputed master of paralysis?

Rumrill said: The man's white van was found wrecked on a road on the outskirts of our town, perhaps near the hospital, collapsed upon or onto or around another car or perhaps a tree or building, and full every inch with unopened, undelivered envelopes and parcels. It was only then that anyone became aware that a significant portion of the town had not received its mail for however many weeks, and only then that they missed it.

He added: Of the man himself, no sign.

Rumrill said: It was clear to me from the manner in which my neighbors told this story that it was to them a parable about the unnatural extremities toward which undisciplined human behavior could aspire. It was clear from the manner in which my neighbors told this story, without sympathy, that it was to them an occasion for mirth.

He added: But, as for myself, my only thought was: *Bruder!*

Rumrill said: And, as for myself, I had my own theory to account for the man's whereabouts. As for myself, I came to believe that the man had ascended or been assumed into the perfection of total ineffectiveness.

He added: Had lain down among our unread, unanswered, unimportant pleas, the spittle that had sealed them, the ink and gum that had anointed them, and been absorbed, bodily, into their communal inconsequence.

Rumrill said: When our town's embarrassed authorities came in time to secretly and in the dead of night dump the entirety of the vanished man's backlog of mail over the side of the Shrieking Bridge, he or what was left of him tumbled into the patient pit along with it, there to putrefy in the damp, be eaten by vermin, be digested and inhaled, be caught up and spun round by the wheels of our electric train. It would be silly to mourn him, I thought, for had he not entered the underworld already a full citizen, passport in hand, free to return whenever the spirit might move him to our little town, there to continue to have no impact on our lives, there to continue to leave no depressions in our snow or mud?

He added: To riot for eternity entirely unnoticed.

Brocklebank writes: Making a successive order out of the surrounding whole, out of totality.

Rumrill said: It was with all this on my mind, I assume, that I came to dream again, that same night, or soon thereafter, of my last day at the library, specifically that, in this iteration of the experience, I stopped off on my way to the subterranean train station in our historic town center to see a new opera that was to be staged by a professional company at our historic town hall. They had traveled all the way to our town from the big city—on the way, I assume, to another big city—and had been trapped unexpectedly within our borders after the gasoline in their trucks had been siphoned out into plastic containers and then absconded with in the night by parties unknown.

He added: Even in my dreams, the best thing would have been to park in one of our handy underground garages.

Rumrill said: The first act of the opera in my dream featured a duet between two friends obliged to say goodbye to one another before one of them—I can't remember which—departs on a long journey. It is a tearful parting.

He added: Mezzo-soprano and tenor.

Rumrill said: One of the two friends asks the other, "Will you come to visit me when I am settled in the place to which I am about to depart?" The other friend reassures the first that yes, a visit is certainly in the cards, that their good-bye is no more permanent or irreversible an adieu than the good-bye one bids to one's bedroom when one closes one's eyes before sleep, or that one bids to the sun when it sets, or that one bids to a mouthful of food when one swallows it.

He added: And so forth.

Rumrill said: The second scene showed let us say the tenor in his new life, which was not noticeably different from the life that he had just left, or pretended to leave, in my dream. He began to sing about his new town, his new occupation, his new love interest, and was thereupon struck down and killed by a car.

He added: A papier-mâché car, in my dream.

Brocklebank writes: With successive evocations each consisting of the same sequence of thematic ideas, but differently proportioned and developed each time.

Rumrill said: It was clear to the audience, however— which is to say to Rumrill, as I watched and listened to the opening aria—that the initial scene was something of a fraud. The tenor had been just a bit too effusive, just a little too anxious to catch his train.

He added: Not electric, but diesel.

Rumrill said: No such reunion would ever have taken place, had the tenor not been killed. He would never have so much as picked up the phone.

He added: The masher.

Rumrill said: Yet the mezzo-soprano left behind couldn't have known that the tenor hadn't been in earnest, nor indeed could she have known that the tenor would soon be incapable of further duplicity. She couldn't have known that he would soon be incapable of anything at all.

He added: Save a protracted descent to the operatic netherworld, backed mainly by woodwinds.

Rumrill said: Ms. Mezzo, in the moment of their duet, had been convinced that this would not be a final farewell. Later on, news of the tenor's death, if it arrived, would not affect this conviction.

He added: And no one alive, in the little world of the opera, was now possessed of the information necessary to prove her wrong.

Rumrill said: Though fraudulent from the get-go, in the moment of the promise, then, the promised duty had been fulfilled. The mezzo-soprano's assumption as to the promise's validity could not help but be the last word on the tenor's trustworthiness, his fidelity.

He added: His character.

Rumrill said: Held in suspension, then, the promised visit would be forever in the subjunctive. The tenor would be, for all intents and purposes, eternally present in the execution of an action he would never have initiated had he lived.

He added: A very practical afterlife.

Brocklebank writes: Seeing cat-ownership as a mathematical/emotional endeavor that uplifts as well as educates.

Rumrill said: On a different unrainy day when Brocklebank, housebound, still remembered his plausible life, he told me, the better to distract me from my intention to escort him outside on his constitutional, that on one of his many supposed trips abroad he had been informed by a flat-chested native woman that the various winds or sorts of wind that blew through this native woman's quaint town—which was, the town, full of "Old World" charm, which charm was easily spotted even from a distance, I was assured—had each been given its own name. "For example," she is supposed to have said to him, "in this adorable little town, to which I am native, a hot steady wind is called X, while a cool intermittent wind Y."

He added: How delightful, I thought.

Rumrill said: How delightful, I thought, to be able to walk oneself up and down the streets of a town where every breath of air has its own identity. I thought, "To walk in a place where every breath of air has its own identity is to walk in a place where not only the geographical but the atmospheric characteristics of the region can be mapped and anticipated along whatever routes one has accustomed oneself to applying one's two feet."

He added: "In whichever order."

Rumrill said: A walk through such a space would be a walk through an environment more personable by far than one in which only the boulevards and buildings and men and women have been assigned proper names or identifying numbers. Raising our veils under the hot X, lifting our collars to keep out the penetrating Y, we would have been *formally introduced* to a greater number of local elements or processes, and would therefore—even as new arrivals, fresh off the bus that runs twice a day to the capital of this country of namers, and whose driver accepts all manner of currency—be more at home in such a place than here, in the town to which we are in reality condemned, in its low and level span of what I have been told was once grassland, where every chance event, such as the intersection of one's route with any old gasp of local air, is nothing more than a run-in with another discourteous yokel.

He added: Best forgotten.

Brocklebank writes: Any bunch of cats inviting a number of possibilities.

Rumrill said: When I tried, however, to picture this country, this utopia where even the breezes line up to be named and blow then by mutual arrangement only at this or that time of year, from this or that direction—even the least-loved and most importunate welcomed with a certain familial deference, even affection—I found I could only envision its avenues as identical to those of our own slack-mouthed and foul-breathed town, with identical façades and culs-de-sac, peopled by identical inhabitants, albeit costumed for the occasion in robes or beads or turbans or berets. When I tried, that is, to enjoy in private the conditions described by Brocklebank in his (successful) attempt to lure Rumrill into a reverie, the better to postpone or perhaps delete from the latter's putative schedule for their day the constitutional the former found in his dotage so insufferable, I visualized for myself not an exotic landscape whose few plausible details might bob for my delectation in the viscous and impenetrable ontological material out of which my feeble imagination on those rare occasions I make demands of it is able to construct this or that lackluster assemblage, but indeed a wholly navigable if stale reproduction of my own habitual routes through our flat and wounded municipality.

He added: What a pisser.

Rumrill said: I wondered what was wrong with me that I could not now at this stage of my decline even manage to fantasize properly about a town, let alone a woman or other windfall, without giving this fantasy the same measurements and smells as the actual town I had been condemned to walk since whatever calamity sent me and my little suitcase hither. I wondered, likewise, whether it was this incapacity in particular that stood in the way of any prospective plans to depart.

He added: Or this incapacity among others.

Brocklebank writes: Retaining the intention as an impetus for further ideas.

Rumrill said: Today it does not surprise me that my mind should have imposed those restrictions upon my putative utopia. Upon what other basis could any fantasy have been founded?

He added: Fabrication is beyond me.

Rumrill said: No wonder that with my eyes closed the patterns I had made with my two feet saw fit to invade the insubstantial map I had hoped to explore, privately, with nothing more than Brocklebank's tantalizations to serve as landscape and cartographer both. No wonder, likewise, that I should see this ideal world of transparency and recognition marred despite it- and myself by the same smuts and erosions visited upon my own sovereign thoroughfares by the other men and women who presume to utilize them.

He added: Without permission.

Rumrill said: Think of the outrages inflicted

upon the predictability of our town as a result of the conduct of the other men and women with whom I was obliged to share it. Men and women, I should add, to whom I have *not* been formally introduced and who often stray across what they could not be aware are the king's roads.

He added: Which is to say, Rumrill's.

Rumrill said: It would be impossible, however, to keep these other men and women away from those routes that, through expediency and habit—or else the obscure pronouncements of some Ur-Rumrill whose instincts or decisions are discernible to myself only in the very selection of said thoroughfares—have come to determine the shape of my progress from house to post office or grocery and then back. And yet even given the statistical likelihood that certain of the other men and women who reside in this town will have utilized an identical route to mine, will have made their ways down what I recognize as one of my own sovereign thoroughfares length for length, exactly as I would have done—or that this *could* happen, or *will* happen, or happen *again*, any moment now—I cannot characterize these accidental emulations of Rumrill as being *trespasses* per se.

He added: Much as I'd like to.

Rumrill said: After all, even an identical and premeditated replication of one of my routes on the part for instance of a Mr. or Mrs. Pickles would fail to incorporate even a fraction of the significance of my movements and in which my movements participate. I can be confident that this is the case given that I myself am unable to recognize the totality of this significance—that is, the entirety of the design, to which my routes contribute their *L* or *O* or *S* shapes day by occasional day.

He added: In cursive, please.

Rumrill said: In a mundane sense, then, I am simply obliged to tolerate the erosion to which my thoroughfares are subjected, no matter how severe— and the offences of our populace range from mild misdemeanors like the cavalier disarrangement of certain newly fallen leaves to capital crimes such as the erection of blockades in the form of abandoned housewares, vehicles, appliances, or relatives, whose appearance in my path might necessitate a course correction, or some other and more dire form of improvisation—if only because the religious and temporal authorities in our town have refused even after repeated petition to police my preferred routes for undesirables. In another, more profound sense, however, I recognize that no such erosion is possible, finally, as my routes can only be my routes when traversed as Rumrill traverses them, in the light of the hidden logic of which they partake.

He added: Whatever that is.

Brocklebank writes: This in keeping with my idea to establish a universe of interchangeable and interlocking structural systems and multiple criteria.

Rumrill said: Certainly I have tried on several occasions to see a logic in my choices of left or right or circle or ellipse. Certainly I have examined—to the degree that they would yield to this interrogation— my memories, and even the maps of our town that were once printed for the use of tourists, inaccurate as experience has proven all of these documents to be, in the hope that I might someday discern the design that would justify my otherwise arcane and circuitous excursions.

He added: Beyond, I mean, my inclination to avoid observation by my fellow citizens.

Brocklebank writes: Tending to take a very practical approach; a cat has certain constraints that have to be dealt with—you can do this, but you can't do that.

Rumrill said: There is something to be said for the notion that our town is itself as unreliable an incorporation in reality as it is in my mind or the minds in toto of all three ex-employees of our defunct Cartographer's Office—or two employees and one comely intern. And I do feel, on occasion, that when my back is turned, our town—like my home, or indeed like Mr. and Mrs. Pickles—is liable to shrink or grow or find itself submerged in who knows what flood tide or firestorm, or overrun by what fearsome mob.

He added: Or a combination thereof.

Rumrill said: I would like to believe that I can't picture this or that exotic locale as different from our town in my fantasies because this town is not my town at all but in fact a sister town in a foreign country, recently devastated, to which I have somehow been removed without my knowledge: gas through the keyhole, a brief tussle with two men in animal masks, then stuffed into a sack that smells of milled rice. It would certainly explain your looks of ruminant incomprehension if I were to find that we are not countrymen at all, that our two languages as well as our respective streets were full of false cognates, such that we inadvertent goodwill ambassadors are continually tantalized by a semblance of intelligible communication or navigation but find ourselves led in no case to our intended destinations.

He added: By whatever routes.

Brocklebank writes: One is always coming back to certain problems.

Rumrill said: Lamentably, as Brocklebank demonstrated to me on so many occasions, to mislead oneself as to the reasons one's life is a shambles, as to the actions one might have avoided to render it less shambolic, in no way ameliorates said shambles. Lamentably, one can concoct and even find evidence for the most outlandish explanations imaginable.

He added: And find your situation little changed.

Rumrill said: This calls to mind the second act of the opera in my dream. It had little to do with the first, explicitly.

He added: My dreams are mine, but do not belong to me.

Rumrill said: In this act, I remember a chorus of men and women portrayed as tailors and mechanics and lawyers and other unremarkable roles. I remember jobs and friendships and scenery and costumes.

He added: And names and responsibilities and routines.

Rumrill said: In this second act, which was a street scene, one of these men with his life of outstanding normality was run down by a car. The accident was rather gruesome, though I only knew this in the way I knew, as the Queen of England, that I could not afford to pay my dinner bill.

He added: In the absence of evidence.

Rumrill said: After the car accident, the opera staged a lovely funeral, which was well attended and very soberly sung. The man who died was married, or else had a loving extended family, or in any case was popular.

He added: Among the quick.

Rumrill said: The next scene in act two was identical to the first—the same street, though dimmer now, the lighting softer, and populated by fewer cast members; the unremarkable roles played by different singers than those who had sung moments before as cobblers and knife-grinders or whatever they might have been in act two, scene one. Again, I mean, it was a city street, with men and women and their lives under the sun: the chorus telling us again about how nice it is to be a carpenter, taxi driver, accountant.

He added: That sort of thing.

Rumrill said: I became uneasy as I noticed that many of these new, unremarkable men and women on the stage were, remarkably, addressing empty air. The stage was sparsely populated, but the unremarkable men and women who occupied it seemed ignorant of the fact that this minor-key reiteration of act two, scene one, was missing most of its participants.

He added: Caps doffed in pantomime, doors held open for nothing and nobody, smiles smiled in silence when an absent performer was meant to sing a solo.

Rumrill said: My unease became fright when I

saw the unremarkable man from act two, scene one walk onstage in the same clothing in which he'd been killed a few minutes earlier. He took up the same position he'd occupied before being run over, and his arrival made at least that one part of the stage sensible again: it transpired that some of the other characters had been in the middle of a conversation with the new arrival, unconcerned that he hadn't, till now, been present to hear what they were saying.

He added: And likewise unsurprised at his advent.

Rumrill said: Other men and women arrived over the course of the scene to take up their positions. The men and women who arrived to take up their positions began to sing without any hesitation, and seemed unaware that there was anything odd in their doing so, that there might be anything odd in the semi-depopulated stage around them.

He added: Which was well decorated by the set dressers of my dream.

Brocklebank writes: My instructional pamphlet *Feeding, Grooming, Exhibition, Temperament, Health, Breeding, 1960 No. 9*, consisting of a straight line drawn on a piece of paper, is to be followed precisely and comes with no instructions.

Rumrill said: Back in the waking world, I tried, perhaps imprudently, certainty hypocritically, to convince Brocklebank that if he would cross the threshold, if he would step into the outdoors with me and take his walk, put one plausible foot in front of the other— or vice versa, should he prefer—he might become *less* rather than more tired, since the tiredness of which he had complained, and that he'd put forward so cleverly to diffuse my intention to make him leave his home, was in my estimation the result of this same refusal, in which he had persisted over so many days, if not weeks, past. His tiredness, I told him, would only become more acute if he stayed in his house today, since it followed that the behavior which had engendered his initial lethargy—whether or not genuine—and which consisted in the main of his stubborn immobility, could only continue to encourage said lethargy (eventually to a point of complete paralysis); while the condition he sought to avoid—namely, motion—would necessarily provoke a different physiological reaction, at variance in all fundamental ways to the conditions that had led us to this impasse.

He added: Succinctly put.

Rumrill said: Brocklebank, on the near side of the door, in yellow, with that bulgy something on his back, near his spine, beneath his sweater, explained to me that his transfer from the state he designated as "in" to that he designated as "out" necessitated the expenditure of no small amount of energy, not to mention fortitude, if one can expend fortitude, which necessities were at present unavailable to him. Indeed, even for Brocklebank to stay "in," he said, required the usage of a certain amount of his limited reserves of energy if its stability as a condition were to be maintained, and a Rumrill simply could not, from his position relative to that of a Brocklebank, ascertain whether or not the pains already taken to successfully stay "in" had left said Brocklebank incapable of a movement "out" without injury.

He added: At last unable to "stay in" *or* "go out."

Brocklebank writes: Having been placed here to distract the intellect and to soothe the senses.

Rumrill said: I came to the conclusion, over our time together, when I had seen and aided the old man at all stages of his daily routine, in every state of dress and un—Brocklebank for his part mercifully spared the humiliations appropriate to his state, given that his state could never achieve a state of proper stateness when his every moment was afloat in the by now neck-high flood of his unmemory—that the thing which had stuck itself to Brocklebank's body, near his kidneys, was a phenomena that only occurred when he was fully dressed. That is, the thing on Brocklebank could only be observed when conditions were such that it could not be properly observed.

He added: Another blow to empiricism.

Rumrill said: No amount of surveillance on my part was sufficient to isolate the moment when his yellow cardigan interacted with the something in question and so resulted in the sight I've noted of a bulge beneath Brocklebank's clothing. I was unable despite my not inconsiderable powers of observation to determine whether the monstrous bulge near Brocklebank's kidneys was a property of Brocklebank himself, or a property of, for instance, his yellow cardigan.

He added: Or a property of the interaction of Brocklebank and said yellow cardigan.

Rumrill said: Not to forget the possibility that the bulge was a property of other elements entirely, elements I was not able to take into account, from my narrow vantage, and which would perhaps reveal the yellow cardigan and even Brocklebank himself as nothing more than incidental, circumstantial, unimportant data in the process of the bulge's manifestation; or at the very least secondary functions not in themselves necessary to the manifestation of the bulge. Perhaps the bulge had always been present in the space now occupied by Brocklebank's house, and, indifferent to our town, its strata of Cambrian, Tertiary, and Cretaceous sediments, its network of concealed tunnels, its pipes and wires, its concrete and tarmacadam and plants in the *Poaceae* family, indifferent even to Brocklebank himself and his yellow cardigan, indifferent to the perceptions of Rumrill, was only made evident by a chance combination of all of these elements, as water might be displaced around an otherwise imperceptible glass thimble dropped into a stream by an itinerant seamstress cursed by a malevolent witch.

He added: Or as a sheet might be displaced by a ghost.

Brocklebank writes: Cat-fancying was quick to turn itself into a commonplace, in hopes of becoming bearable.

Rumrill said: As though I had been contaminated by contact with the space that the so-called bulge meant to occupy—or else, as though in punishment for my treatment of the old man—my own "condition" worsened to the point of crisis after Brocklebank's death, and the loss of Brocklebank's supposedly more substantial demesne. Now that I was able to afford my own home, a home that need not be shared with neighbors or their talk, a home from which the new buildings in this town could not be seen, it only became more difficult to bear the notion that, in the absence of my perception of it, my refuge might disappear or cease.

He added: To have something of one's own is in this sense far worse than dispossession.

Rumrill said: This fear had always been in my mind, whether I was at my post at the public library, located in our historic town center, or else on the electric train midway over the Shrieking Bridge, flanked by women in shamelessly colored scarves; or indeed buttonholed in Brocklebank's foyer, engaged in my hunt for a glimpse of his lump. But that *my house* in particular might become an abstraction—compressed for space in my memory, made into a pastiche or parody or impression of itself, as my coworkers at the library had pastiched or parodied myself, for example, and vice versa—was intolerable.

He added: And robbed my possession of pleasure and utility.

Rumrill said: I needed to know that my home was present and continuous in order for myself to apprehend the world outside my house with any clarity, or, to be honest, courage. Which is to say, the knowledge that I can return to my home makes the world outside my house navigable, not only in a geographical sense— in that I know where I am in relation to my home and know what route I would need to take in order to return there—but in the more significant sense that a house to return to makes the world outside that house comprehensible: characterized, I mean, as an interruption in my presence there.

He added: There, in safety.

Rumrill said: Given this inability to believe that things in the world persist in my absence in the same way that they persist when I'm present to perceive them, it follows that, in order for my house to be present and continuous, I would need to be nearby to see it as such. That is, in order to know that I have a home to return to, in order to be safely in the world outside my home, I would need to be *in* my home.

He added: Consternation.

Rumrill said: Indeed, I had in my youth tried many times to resolve this difficulty. My failures were numerous enough that I had by this time come to consider it insoluble.

He added: Without, I mean, a second Rumrill handy.

Rumrill said: I tested a number of interim solutions over the years before I managed to settle at last on a prospect rugged enough to withstand the swells of implausibility the big world likes so much to send my way, and so see my little ship capsize. These measures weren't initiated in a spirit of scientific inquiry, but were desperate improvisations, necessitated by the need to find and retain employment, so called, in this town, whether in the service of a library or a Brocklebank, and so be furnished with capital sufficient to attend to quotidian anxieties such as debts and the removal or excavation respectively by our town doctor of cysts and fistulae; and perhaps even—I might at various stages have hoped—marriage and cohabitation with a woman who would if not innovate upon then simply duplicate the ministrations once performed on my behalf by the woman in the stacks; and all in all lead what we might call a full and satisfactory life in the big world along with my fellow human beings.

He added: Of whom, thankfully, there seem to be fewer and fewer.

Rumrill said: All of these attempted reconciliations of my condition might be said to belong to one of two categories: formal or concrete. Formal solutions were internal, so to speak, cerebral: different manners of thought with regard to my condition such that I hoped would circumvent what is even to myself recognizable as an irrational phobia with no basis in fact; whereas concrete solutions involved practical manipulations of my environment or the people who saw fit to clutter said environment, in order to effect a similar cure.

He added: Or, better put, "a similar means by which to outmaneuver my condition, if only for a short time."

Rumrill said: I might also characterize these as "soft" and "hard" solutions, respectively. Or else, we might say "persiflage" and "slapstick."

He added: Comic in either case.

Brocklebank writes: Realizing that the unprecedented divergence between contemporary cat-fancying and its adherents on the one hand and traditional pet-ownership and its following on the other is not accidental and most probably not transitory, but rather that it is a result of a half-century of revolution in thought, a revolution whose nature and consequences can be compared only with, and in many respects are closely analogous to, those of the mid-nineteenth-century evolution in theoretical physics, the immediate and profound effect has been the necessity of the informed cat owner to reexamine and probe the very foundations of his art.

Rumrill said: An example of a soft—indeed the softest—solution would have been to simply ignore my anxiety, in the hope that I would eventually acclimatize myself to whatever new environment I needed to occupy despite the suspicion, or sensation, that my home, somewhere behind me, over the bridge, was no longer extant. This was effective in the short term, in the early days of my illness, so long as I was able to bear in mind that I would return home at such and such a time, without fail, and could think of no particular reason I might be detained.

He added: Fire, flood, famine.

Rumrill said: Another example of a soft solution would be to decide that whatever location I might find myself in at the end of whatever journey I'd undertaken outside my home would be, now, a new home—if a less comfortable and satisfactory home— for whatever length of time I would have to occupy said location. Further to this ploy, I would familiarize myself as much as possible with these interim locations or landscapes so as to allow me to make the same kinds of observation—albeit in a markedly shallow register—as would occupy me in my home: for example, the number of footsteps from my chair to the bathroom door, or in what corners dust tends most to collect, or the painted-over water damage over my bed resembling nothing so much as the continent of Australia.

He added: What we might call the "quirks" or "personality" of a location, not architecturally, or not *only* architecturally, but on the level of day-to-day, eye-level perception.

Rumrill said: I spent a good deal of time in minute scrutiny, for instance, of the public library, where I was obliged for some years to work eight hours a day away from my home—though my home then was a different home than the one I occupy now, a fact that made my absence from it easier to bear, since the prospective loss of that location in particular would not have been irreparable.

He added: Nor would I have begrudged the void my many fellow tenants.

Rumrill said: I attempted to cultivate this kind of relationship not only with the library itself, and its stacks and desks and offices and carpets and bathrooms (upstairs and down), but with the route between my then-home and the library, which was invariable. That is, I tried to cultivate the same level of attention as far as the streets that led from my then-home to the train, and as far the train itself, and as far as the concrete meridians and lampposts, left and right, upon the Shrieking Bridge, each fitted with its life preserver and placard stamped with words to the effect that life is too precious to be thrown away, please use the phone below to call for help; as far too as the walk from the station, which in our historic downtown is located underground, up its tiled and mildewy staircase to the air, and thence to our library located between so many shuttered rustic shopfronts, etc.

He added: Or do I mean *usw.*

Brocklebank writes: Many of my so-called

instructions being impossible for other fanciers to realize, perhaps including myself now, because the past ten years have changed my physiognomy and psychology.

Rumrill said: In the end, however, an incident on the train, on my way home on my last and suspiciously eventful day at the library, convinced me that this "soft" solution would not be a viable foundation upon which I might base a lifetime of free movement up or down our streets or really to any point on the compass. I was forced on that day by the volume of passengers in the train car I had been unlucky enough to select to sit in an aisle seat, which I found most distasteful.

He added: The window seat occupied by a young lady in a shrilly colored scarf.

Rumrill said: After only a minute it seemed to me that she had her eyes fixed shamelessly on my poor posture as I tried to give the impression that I had not noticed her attentions. It unnerved me.

He added: Not that it takes much.

Rumrill said: Yet it's rather unusual for a passenger who has been forced to share her row with a stranger to stare so conspicuously at her chance companion. It is most particularly unusual for a passenger in our town to do so in the brief period of time that her train car spends in the open air, when it emerges from the ancient tunnels into which it had descended because obliged by its fixed route to cross the property contiguous with our historic town center, through which no tracks could be laid; when it rises, I mean, in triumph for the span of a single bridge into the sun or moonlight.

He added: Before it is then consigned again to

the depths so as not to inconvenience the ears of our residential neighborhoods.

Rumrill said: It is most particularly unusual because tradition dictates that passengers make use of this apotheosis to avail themselves of the nearest window to stare out over or into our town and its buildings, which, before the advent of your tenements, as I've mentioned, had been congregated entirely below this altitude, such that a ride over our little bridge was the only opportunity to take in the "view," so called, as one was carried safely from one shore to another of our famous railway graveyard—a trench or fen that the bridge was built to traverse, in which partially digested Pullman cars and Bakelite radio sets can to this day be seen submerged at unlikely angles in the silt—the view, that is, of our massed businesses, public-works projects, rotted factories, and muddy parks, not to mention the squat residences that were built adjacent to this wilderness, as though it were a river from which they might draw sustenance and not a canker from which prehistoric piston oil still leaks into our ground water. Tradition also dictates that one or more mordant remarks are made on each such journey with regard to the lampposts that appear at regular intervals on either side of the bridge, along the narrow ledge reserved for human traffic, each pole host to a lifesaver hung from a L-shaped hook, as well as a telephone receiver linked directly to a sister receiver, red in color, located at our fire department; these along with weathered cards printed with mottos contra the use of our town's once-highest edifice for the purposes of *Selbtsmord*.

He added: Short though the drop must be.

Rumrill said: (I haven't been back to the Bridge since the day I dumped Brocklebank's books. Which I deposited there not for revenge's sake, I should say, but because of the tiny white wormlike insects I had seen efface the ligature in an *Eszett* one afternoon.)

He added: (Under a very red sunset.)

Rumrill said: I came to the conclusion, as regarded the scarf lady's unselfconscious regard, that she was interested not in the eccentric older man seated by her right elbow but in something visible to her in the row opposite, past me, perhaps a friend or an especially eccentric vagrant. To the young lady in the scarf, I was no more than a volume of space empty of matter—anyway filled with nothing worth note—through which she could gawk without embarrassment.

He added: Transparent Rumrill.

Rumrill said: Yet, after several more minutes of this, and after our train had again returned to the dark, I was forced to reexamine my hypothesis. The young lady in her shameless scarf could now have with greater ease and comfort kept the opposite side of the car under observation via the window to which she was directly adjacent—thanks I mean to the properties of light upon semitransparent, reflective surfaces.

He added: Famous worldwide.

Rumrill said: That is, she need not have turned her head at all, since in the unlit subway tunnels beneath our town, the lightless windows functioned as mirrors of their cars' lit interiors. If she had wanted to keep the row opposite surveilled, she need not have exerted herself even so far as turning her head, nor left herself vulnerable in this way to my misinterpretation of her stare.

He added: As brazen in her gape as her scarf was in color.

Rumrill said: I was forced to conclude that the apparent disregard of myself exhibited by the young lady in the scarf was itself a ruse. That her studious disregard of myself was intended to allay any suspicion on my part that I might be under observation for purposes unknown.

He added: But, as purposes go, probably sinister.

Rumrill said: I knew from my own experience as a window-seat occupant that the one thing in a train carriage that it's impossible to see reflected in its windows while said car is in an unlit tunnel is, precisely, the person sitting directly adjacent to you. Whether you lean forward or lean back, the only thing you can see at that angle in a subway window is your own face.

He added: With carbon copies on pink onionskin.

Rumrill said: I knew this because there had been many occasions on which I'd been curious to know who was seated next to me on the train, on a given day, when I was myself the one trapped, as it were, on the interior of the row, in the window seat; which was, despite this sense of restraint, my preferred position, for reasons that remain obscure to me. To turn my head in order to look directly at the object of my curiosity, who was perhaps a comely woman—to stare at my neighbor, that is, as the young lady in the scarf felt empowered to do qua Rumrill, whatever her motive—would surely have attracted his or her attention.

He added: And the railroad cops have only so much patience.

Rumrill said: Given these compunctions, I was usually unable to satisfy my curiosity and form any clear picture of the person next to me. As far as gender, facial structure, or even clothing, I was left unilluminated, save perhaps when they rose at last and departed.

He added: And sometimes not even then.

Rumrill said: On the day in question, though, the young lady's apparently vacant stare was far more complex and subtle a phenomenon than I'd initially assumed, I now assumed. On our departure from the station nearest the public library, it may indeed have been the case that her eyes had been fixed not on Rumrill but on the row opposite—maybe she was a recent detainee in our town (or had been instructed to operate under this pretense), and so found (or pretended to find) the spikier convolutions of our train cars' brass fittings to be of some historical interest.

He added: Inconvenient though they are to hang from should no seats be available.

Rumrill said: In time, however, I theorized, her attention had been caught by Rumrill's noble deportment, and for the brief moments of our ascent toward the air and then traversal of our bridge, her stare was every bit as audacious as I've described. "Here," she thought, "sits a legitimate native of this town, the apogee of its cultural and intellectual progress, the solution to its riddles, the victim of its influence."

He added: Largely ceremonial.

Rumrill said: As our train returned once more to its stygian habitat, however, she realized that she had been too obvious in her appraisal of Rumrill's profile, and so turned her eyes to the window parallel our row so as not to seem to stare. Thanks to the darkness of the tunnels outside, of course, these far windows reflected none other than Rumrill.

He added: At her elbow.

Rumrill said: All this I intuited in a flash and wondered then at the subtlety with which this observer—casual, or under the instructions of who knows what power—had played out her stratagem. She had moved from one legitimate or sham object of observation to another, all without the least movement of her head, with never a doubt that Rumrill would be at work all this while to decipher her intentions.

He added: His own head likewise stock-still.

Brocklebank writes: My system being a combination structural platform that establishes terms and particulars for creative participation.

Rumrill said: The young woman and her scarf exited the train three stops past where I would myself ordinarily have stepped out onto the platform in order to climb again into the air and begin my walk from station to home, but which, embroiled in our oblique stare-down and my analysis of same, I had today allowed to sail past as though just another anonymous island of light on the electric train's tireless circumnavigation of our town, of no more interest than those stations contiguous to neighborhoods now uninhabitable due to fire or flood, or in any case inhabited by no one of interest. The ramifications of this were more terrible than mere absentmindedness.

He added: And more terrible too than the probably dangerous walk home through the sunset-colored streets that led back to Rumrill's proper milieu among his coevals in the middle or lower-middle classes.

Rumrill said: What use, I asked myself, as I trudged home afraid, was it for me to cultivate the same level of attention as far as the train, as far as whatever landmarks might be found along my route, as far as the concrete meridians and lampposts, left and right, on the Shrieking Bridge, as far as the eyes and scarves and lips of the bystanders or –sitters encountered along my route, if my appreciation of these details only caused me to develop, if in a shallower register, because of my observations, because of the observations in turn inflicted upon me by any passersby, by any fellow commuters, the same inertia with regard to these supposedly unimportant, impermanent, interim locations, when the time came to depart them, as I did leaving my home?

He added: What a pisser.

Rumrill said: Despite the library or the train or the train station or the grocery or the post office's expendability, to my eyes, in comparison with my then-home (and certainly with my house today), such that their ingestion by the void should not have caused me any more grief than the gradual elimination of the preterite tense in a language I've never learned, the more attention and respect I invested in these places, the more they became inhabitable for me—became storied, that is, in my memory, after the inculcation by what I am pleased to call the *Weltanschauung* of Rumrill of their details, of their delectable specificity; for instance as regards in which corner this or that carpet had hidden its most intricate fray, or by which water fountain it was possible to hear the less potable variety of water coming out of the women balanced above the bowls in the nearby library restroom, or for example any of the numerous peripeteia involved in the observation of a woman in a shrill scarf on one's daily commute, of the observation of her reflection or my own reflection in the observation of the other's observing reflection—the more I found myself reluctant or even unable to depart them and so leave them to their fates. Every location or landscape I might traverse or inhabit often enough to grow familiar with or interested in their many plausible details might well become, I saw—as had my home—the locus of the same disinclination to *move*.

He added: Might become, in their way, semi-precious.

Rumrill said: Left unchecked, my attention, loosed upon the big world and reflected back by the attentions of women in shrill scarves, would in time leave me unable even to transition from a state of stillness to a state of motion, or vice versa—and wherever I might be, along one of my sovereign thoroughfares—without the same terrible fear I experienced when it was necessary that I leave my home. No exceptional insight is required to see that this condition of total acceptance of the big world and so total immobility would have to be reckoned worse than the one I had employed this "soft" solution to alleviate.

He added: Total stasis.

Rumrill said: It could likewise be reckoned "worse" because in order to put an end to the anxiety generated by this new predicament—or metastasization of my original predicament—I would need not a single duplicate Rumrill with which to "anchor" my home, but an endless supply of doubles held in permanent reserve to scatter in my path and then instruct to sit in indefinitely prolonged observation of the locations or landscapes in which I'd planted them, to allow the primary me (which is to say, Rumrill) to continue his progress toward whatever goal. It could likewise be reckoned "worse" because it feels to me that the necessity for an endless supply of Rumrills is somehow more impossible than the necessity for a single duplicate.

He added: Though of course these are equally impossible.

Brocklebank writes: Seeing much of my early work as dealing with cats as a physical presence, sculpting them, building up layers in complex constructions.

Rumrill said: An example of a *hard* solution would be the arrangement of certain conditions in my home to serve as an *aide-mémoire*, or should I say *Gedächtnisstütze*, in the visualization of whatever it might be that I felt so certain would no longer be present in the world when I was unavailable to perceive it personally, and whose absence would cause me such anxiety. This term is not wholly appropriate, however, since my memory, which always and effortlessly records the minutia of a given environment without the need for artificial props or accessories or reminders, is perfectly sound, indeed superior.

He added: Better, then, to say *aide-être*, or do I mean *Daseinstütze*.

Rumrill said: I didn't need help to remember

how my apartment or house was or is disposed. I needed help to believe that they existed.

He added: A question of conviction, not recollection.

Rumrill said: An example of a hard solution of the *Daseinstütze* type would be to leave my kitchen tap in the on position. To leave my tap in the on position would be to begin an indisputable and continuous event that would proceed in my absence and so help me to visualize my home too as indisputable and continuous.

He added: Organized around a particular source of anxiety.

Rumrill said: Another example of a hard solution of the *Daseinstütze* type would be to leave my front door unlocked or indeed ajar in invitation to some especially eccentric vagrant. In competition with the primary anxiety of nonexistence, these distraction anxieties might prove very helpful to someone (which is to say, Rumrill) nominally convinced of the unreality of the location in which they would occur.

He added: Few fires or floods or invasions are reported of nonexistent homes, to my knowledge.

Rumrill said: Another example of a hard solution of the *Daseinstütze* type would be the placement of a series of more or less inconspicuous mirrors to reflect a portion of the exterior of my home to me even at great distances. By "great distances" I mean only a length of our ex-prairieland as might be comfortably tilled by one man behind one ox in the course of one day, given that the exigencies of arranging such an apparatus over distances greater than such was entirely beyond me.

He added: And I felt that it would demean me to bring in an outside contractor.

Brocklebank writes: Working nonetheless with reduced means.

Rumrill said: Toward the end of our relationship, as I am pleased to call it, I began to wonder whether it was not possible that my indifference—my passive interference, my unmalicious sabotage, attributable, I speculate, to my resentment of the old man's niggling cruelties, or else my preoccupation with the woman in the stacks, she long since gone by this time (by this time herself between the cars of an unelectric train on the hinterlands of a city I could not imagine save as a version, larger and in a different hue, sprinkled with minarets perhaps, of our own little town, with its ancient electric commuter rail, which rattles in 4/4 time as it crosses the Shrieking Bridge; unlike this foreign train, imaginary, over some other sort of bridge, likewise imaginary, whose rattles come in 7/8), likely engaged in activities with a stranger or strangers that I could and cannot imagine save as versions, more vigorously rhythmic, of what she and I once rehearsed in that section of our library consecrated to books on Byzantine architecture—whether my lack of attention, I mean, to the words Brocklebank intended for me to type and then file away in the metal cabinets that I have, like his cats, either inherited or reconstructed, was itself the fatal gap, the point of infection, by means of which the emptiness that had waited so patiently for a chance to return to Brocklebank's life—return from its exile in Istanbul, perhaps, to which it had been condemned by the composition of his tortuous procedures—came at last to regain its foothold in his home, and so work, just as systematically, to spider into and make null everything that had once seemed solid to him. While he dictated, I would stare out the sole window in Brocklebank's study at a sky filled with neither clouds nor blue, only to set down in my own good time who knows what sort of incidental flotsam might have come into my head, listening to that cane-husk voice swish and chafe both my own two ears and the walls' however-many.

He added: Ears, I mean.

Rumrill said: If I had been hired to be Brocklebank's *Gedächtnisstütze*, was it not possible that my failure or refusal to record his words had caused or encouraged the condition that led in time to his being unable to remember anything other than those words I had—badly and inaccurately—recorded? Had I murdered Brocklebank, mind and body, with my unconcern?

He added: If, after all, it wasn't his forgetfulness I was hired to document.

Brocklebank writes: Evenings, reading my cats to sleep, trying to capture, for each character in the story, an individual and consistent vocal behavior; and they being demanding critics, stimulating a good deal of nocturnal reflection about vocal identity.

Rumrill said: His recitations continued daily until his death. Since he could now only consult his original notes and then my own transcriptions of his opus, and since the latter now far outnumbered the former, his thoughts became more and more muddied, until the signal-to-noise ratio was weighted entirely in favor of noise.

He added: Gobbledygook become gibberish, if you like.

Brocklebank writes: Asking, is a stabbing pain like being stabbed, a burning one as when one is burned, a drawing pain like being drawn, pulled?

Rumrill said: On a day when my employer still remembered his wife, he told me the story of how she and he had reacted to the news, conveyed by our neighborhood doctor, that she would not live to see the end of whatever season it then was when she and he had wended down their sovereign thoroughfares to his (the doctor's) examination room. The Brocklebanks had walked through the snow or dandelions to consult the doctor on the subject of those pains that then occurred with some regularity in whatever part of Mrs. Brocklebank's body and of which she had cause lately to complain.

He added: Or do I need to slow down.

Rumrill said: Husband and wife removed their boots at the boot-check in the doctor's anteroom, a space sunk the depth of an upright man into the ground, this upright man's head at the level perhaps of the second internode of an immature *Taraxacum*, and in which a collection of other white- or red-faced townspeople were already seated in the smell of worms and melted ice. Doctors are privileged to enter into contact with all strata of society, grouped as it is in large part into families of different sizes, possessed of bank accounts of different sizes, and checkbooks imprinted with all manner of watermark: three surmullets, perhaps, at gaze gules.

He added: A fish used, I've read, as a primitive sort of television by the ancient Romans, on account of the many vibrant colors it turned as it suffocated and expired in the air.

Rumrill said: Our town doctor, I suppose of a mind to observe the colors Mrs. Brocklebank might herself turn as she expired, agreed to see her ahead of the other citizens in his anteroom, other patients who had been there longer but whose families were not yet friendly—or not yet friendly enough—with their friendly GP: a man in late middle age whose kited, crenellated ears these recent initiates into the ranks of the unwell found amusing, which fact they marshaled the vigor to comment upon even as they felt their *vis vitalis* sapped by whatever symptoms they had trekked through our lurid streets to ask said comically eared physician to diagnose. Seated and frustrated with the sight of Mrs. Brocklebank ushered with conciliation into the examination room when by all rights they— these other patients—should have preceded her, the townspeople scowled through their rheum in piqued accusation of the husband, abandoned, as he brushed or rebrushed the snow or pollen stains off of his two boots.

He added: With an East Coast newspaper.

Rumrill said: The doctor in no time pronounced Mrs. Brocklebank to be host to a disorder not uncommon whose name and other particulars escape me. He told her, in short, that the processes that constituted Mrs. Brocklebank, citizen and organism, had in their wisdom and for a change of pace decided to leave off their usual obligations and turn instead to the

ingestion of this same Mrs. Brocklebank—a decision
not at all characteristic of said processes, given that
the perpetuation of precisely this Mrs. Brocklebank
had been their one notable responsibility to date—
and then build with those resources that had once
been devoted to Brocklebankian continuity some
other item or function or entity that, unhappily, was
not quite the triumph of design that was our Mrs.
Brocklebank, whatever her flaws, not least her hideous
feet, and would therefore in its construction end with
the probably unintentional murder-suicide of both the
tenuous concatenation still named, despite this meta-
morphosis, "Mrs. Brocklebank" (and which would,
tragically, remain enough of a Mrs. Brocklebank
throughout the procedure to be aware of and suffer
through the untenability of this incomplete and ill-
considered reconfiguration of said resources), as well
as those very systems that had decided, for reasons of
their own, to undertake this desperate improvisation.

He added: And which could not be reasoned
with.

Rumrill said: How she did weep, I assume, this
Mrs. Brocklebank, albeit without the awareness that
this lamentation was itself a byproduct of those processes that had by then long since embarked down
their sovereign thoroughfares upon the great adven-
ture of her decease. How she did wail at the same picture window where later I would myself look out at
the street to watch the poplars smolder.

He added: Myself in attendance at her husband's
own inelegant disintegration.

Brocklebank writes: Not once is ordinary fancying "fancying."

Rumrill said: After the doctor had given this news to Mrs. Brocklebank, and she had passed it along, perhaps with subtle modifications, to her husband, he no longer (the doctor) seemed a friend of the family but a technician tasked only with the clear articulation of protocol to a successor. Since Mrs. Brocklebank *qua* Mrs. Brocklebank would have no further need of doctors, she no longer fell within the doctor's purview, and so was of little interest to a man the majority of whose many friends were still alive.

He added: And might for some time yet be kept in this condition.

Rumrill said: Soon Mr. and Mrs. Brocklebank came to see that, having no relations alive between our neighborhood and Istanbul, there would be little profit in the pretense that Mrs. Brocklebank might continue to be a matter worth Mr. Brocklebank's or indeed our mayor or grocer's attention after her paraphrase, so to speak, from this town and world. They decided, husband and wife, that they would mourn her together there and then, while both were alive to enjoy it, rather than wait until this bereavement became a performance—symbolic, operatic—given by one person (Mr. B.) for no audience.

He added: If "enjoy" is the word.

Rumrill said: They removed Mrs. Brocklebank's name from the shared bank account into which their life savings had been deposited, and which they were allowed by their bank's board of trustees to visit at given times on work days, a privilege that stands as a clear demonstration of the board's great good will toward its clients. The Brocklebanks then filed whatever paperwork was necessary at our town hall to have their car registered in his name alone.

He added: If they had a car.

Rumrill said: They did what they could to act together as though Mrs. Brocklebank had not only received a death sentence from her doctor but had died there and then, and so had in the meantime taken her place in a hereafter that resembled nothing so much as precisely the same sights, sounds, expectations, and substances she would soon, in her coffin, or on her bier, relinquish. Mrs. Brocklebank was in fact suspended in an interregnum that could with accuracy be described as a life after death.

He added: A very practical afterlife.

Rumrill said: This period seemed to Mr. Brocklebank very fine, until he forgot it. Until he forgot it, he often referred to this period as their happiest together.

He added: As a family.

Rumrill said: The Brocklebanks made the best of death, you see, inasmuch as it helped them to reconcile to one another, to become more efficient in their interaction, to appreciate one another, to mend fences, build bridges, and other no doubt significantly architectural turns of phrase beloved of Mrs. Brocklebank. The nothing that had in health been a burden for them to express one to the other now in sickness became a pleasure.

He added: Though substantially the same nothing.

Brocklebank writes: The variation of the features of a basic unit producing all the thematic formulations which provide for fluency, contrasts, variety, logic, and unity, on the one hand, and character, mood, expression, and every needed differentiation on the other.

Rumrill said: Brocklebank had already retired from watch-repair by the time his wife was diagnosed. His wife, however, who was younger than he, continued to hold a job for several years after they had relocated to our town, and so left their house on average once per day and then returned to it usually in the evening.

He added: An equivalent number of times.

Rumrill said: Since I was never told what it was exactly that Mrs. Brocklebank worked at, in the days she worked, we might for the sake of argument say that she was employed at an institution with whose workings I am familiar. My imagination, such as it is, can only stretch so far, and a painter of lacquer pen boxes would fall well beyond its purview.

He added: So, a librarian.

Rumrill said: But it isn't as important to know what she did for her livelihood or distraction as it is important for us to understand that Mrs. Brocklebank would because of her employment have had ample opportunity before her virtual and actual demises to make new friends while she was away from her house, on her way to or from her job, or indeed *at* her job, for she must have had coworkers, perhaps friendly, perhaps not too dissimilar from those whose companies I was myself obliged to enjoy under the same or similar light fixtures. Mrs. Brocklebank might, for instance, before her pre-mortem reconciliation with her mister, have met a person with whom she could have carried out, if that's the term—possessed, inculcated, digested?—an extramarital affair, due why else to the not-inconsiderable friction between herself and her stopped-watch husband, from whom she had only grown more distant as the years distanced them from their courtship on what amounted to another planet.

He added: Namely, Vienna.

Rumrill said: We know nothing about this putative lover of Mrs. Brocklebank save the degree of his or her likelihood, which would be a nice big high-rise of red on the bar graph I did not prepare to illustrate this point. Yet, by way of visual aids, it may be that I still have in my archives a sample of this hypothetical lothario's rather impressive handwriting, which in its grace of line and proud but not ostentatious flourishes might remind us of a medieval copyist's, executed in the light of whatever flamboyant and unintimidated sky would have been evident through his cell's single window, hay dust insinuated into this close atmosphere by a poorly stuffed mattress, its innards partially prolapsed onto the floor, which is to say the loose and rounded cobbles our monk's weak ankles daily essayed as they wobbled to and fro on necessary errands away from his bench with chorales of no less than fifteen cartilaginous clicks.

He added: Each.

Rumrill said: Unlettered Mrs. Brocklebank wrote letters to her friend, poorly, about mundane matters: stomach pains, sleeplessness, financial anxieties, and so forth. Her letters touched, that is, on matters typical for a husband and wife to discuss, had diplomatic relations not been cut off.

He added: And the embassies abandoned.

Rumrill said: That the content of Mrs. Brocklebank's letters did not in itself seem to cry out, especially, for concealment behind the green radiator where I later found them, might lead us to deduce, for one, that Mr. and Mrs. Brocklebank—before her abrupt gradation from civil to astronomical twilight, if I may put it that way—spoke to one another very little about such mundane matters as would not otherwise be untypical to touch upon in casual conversation with one's spouse. For another, that Mrs. Brocklebank and this probable extramarital person were intimate enough to find it commonplace to discuss between them such mundane matters as would not otherwise be untypical in what daily talk must occur I assume between a husband and wife.

He added: With carbon copies on pink onionskin.

Rumrill said: We need not refrain from the pleasure of further surmises, given the content of Mrs. Brocklebank's radiator letters; for example that said letters or copies of drafts of letters had been hidden not because of their content, which after all was so innocuous as to frustrate any malevolent misreading we might want to imagine for them; not, that is, because there was any fear in Mrs. B's heart that the neat little characters in red ink now static between those spongy, inoffensive strands of processed linen (suspiciously unsinged after who knows how many winters' worth of Brocklebankian steam heat) might be read by her husband. No, they must have been hidden (if indeed they were hidden and not, say, lost) specifically because of the intimacy the letters implied must exist between Mrs. Brocklebank and her correspondent: devoted as those letters were to such nugatory matters as the progress of her radish crop in the backyard garden and then the inexplicable dreams she'd been having about nonexistent operas and the persistent, worrying pains she had begun to feel in this or that quadrant of her Austrian body and which she had not yet confessed to her perhaps autistic husband.

He added: (Or presumed husband.)

Rumrill said: Perhaps the letters had initially been kept in Mrs. Brocklebank's drop-front secretary along with her other, less incriminating correspondence. Perhaps Mr. Brocklebank on a routine inspection of his wife's papers had read through these letters, and had taken up the matter with his wife, indelicately, and only then did she hide them, in retaliation for his trespass, or simply in order that any additional letters which might be added to the cache would remain confidential, safe behind the green radiator.

He added: Or "safe."

Rumrill said: Then again, as Mr. Brocklebank never struck me as the sort of man who would confront his wife directly with evidence of her putative infidelity, particularly if discovered in this manner, Mrs. Brocklebank would probably have needed to figure out for herself that her privacy, so called, had been invaded. But Mr. Brocklebank would not, I suspect, have been the sort of person possessed of a memory so precise as to be able to return his wife's most dear and secret things to within a centimeter of their initial placement.

He added: Even in those days in need of an amanuensis.

Rumrill said: Brocklebank always struck me, rather, as the sort of man who, in preference to an open confrontation, would give his wife (or employee) sharp jabs, *little hints* that he had discovered in their initial or perhaps second or seventh hiding place documents in support of the likelihood that certain indiscretions, be they amorous or financial, had transpired. I imagine that he committed to his admittedly wobbly if by contrast robust memory certain phrases from his wife's letters, and then integrated these into his daily conversations with her on matters certainly no less quotidian than adultery but demonstrably of greater utility in their household—for instance the replenishment of their stock of rye bread and whitefish salad—so as to make evident to her, albeit without her recognition of this fact—no more, really, than a sense of disquiet—that he, Brocklebank, knew all.

He added: Though in reality he only knew that there was something to know.

Rumrill said: I would go on to imagine that Mrs. Brocklebank never did notice her husband's little hints, not even un- or sub- or sur- or preconsciously. I would imagine, instead, that the old man's plan miscarried, since, subjected to this use of her own words "against her," Mrs. Brocklebank would most likely have found Mr. Brocklebank in fact marginally more agreeable than he ordinarily, at this time, was.

He added: More agreeable and more intelligible.

Rumrill said: And then, after some time had passed—enough for Mr. Brocklebank to see that his clever effort to undermine his wife's confidence had been entirely ineffective—he even began to find that many of the purloined words and phrases he'd designated as *little hints* had spontaneously, and without his permission, infiltrated what he would before have considered his normal mode of discourse. For instance, if his wife had in one of her letters to her mysterious admirer made mention of a "lovely sunset"—whatever that means—Brocklebank himself now discovered that he had moved, and without any awareness of the transition, from the employment of such a phrase in spite to its use in inadvertent earnest.

He added: "From the window they saw together the lovely jade sunset behind the trees."

Rumrill said: Brocklebank had made another unpleasant discovery, namely that there is no difference between the ironic emulation of a mode of thought and its development, as it were, naturally. One day, then, when he had found that he could no longer distinguish between the words he had assimilated from his wife's thin blue airmail paper and the words he had till that time collected and deployed in the ordinary, unmalicious course of his life, he decided to return to the drop-front secretary to which he had restored Mrs. Brocklebank's letters after he had assimilated them, in order to remind himself, through further study, just which of these habitual words and phrases had come from Mrs. Brocklebank and which from sources by contrast natural and guiltless.

He added: But the letters were gone.

Rumrill said: Brocklebank despaired that there would be no other way to cleanse his mind of the blue airmail words. "This Brocklebank," thought Brocklebank, "the Brocklebank I have become, is no longer the Brocklebank of old, but a Brocklebank in whose libretto are included those words once hidden not especially well in my wife's desk."

He added: Inasmuch as the new Brocklebank could remember the old Brocklebank with any clarity.

Rumrill said: Brocklebank wouldn't have given up, though; he would have innovated some way to purge himself of the words and thereby the thoughts and thereby the associations and interpretations and conclusions that he had so precipitately imbibed from the blue airmail paper—and which were now, unknown or perhaps unbeknownst to him, hidden behind the nearby and we must infer rather inefficient green radiator. He probably recognized that the only path open to him was to attempt to compose and then utilize as the required baseline a *reconstruction* of the letters (to the best of his memory) rather than the repurloined originals; to which end Brocklebank sat down one day at his wife's drop-front secretary while she was away at work, and, finding her stock of blue airmail paper, used one of his wife's red pens to begin his purification.

He added: Nothing simpler.

Rumrill said: He began tentatively, with the sorts of thing he supposed a first letter from his wife to her friend might contain. This letter would be necessarily guarded and unconfident.

He added: Timid.

Rumrill said: What things Brocklebank's wife and her friend had *gotten up to* together—perhaps, thought Brocklebank, in the very stacks of the library where she then worked—to warrant the net gain in intimacy that manifested itself over the course of Mrs. Brocklebank's one-sided correspondence needed to be decided upon in advance, by Brocklebank, if he meant to redraft the letters properly. What had gone on in Vienna in the years between two famous wars between many famous countries between our Mr. Brocklebank and a woman who would for reasons of her own thereafter sign away the surname given her by her parents—themselves spared the bother of growing sick and senile thanks to the expediency of murder—what went on, I mean, in these circumstances between two young Austrians, reckless, huddled together on a street I would not recognize at an hour I am not often awake to see, though perhaps interrupted before consummation (in the legal sense) by a policeman who thereupon showed them much unearned kindness (permission granted for them, dishabille, to return to their two family homes without official reprimand for this violation of the ordinance or ordinances contra public indecency)—this, then, represented the limits of what Brocklebank could imagine that his once-comely wife and her friend at the library had *got up to* in the stacks.

He added: Pretty tame stuff.

Rumrill said: Mr. Brocklebank returned many times to his wife's desk to perfect with her ink pens and upon her preferred stationary the phrases he hoped would in time return his vocabulary and therefore habits of mind and therefore behavior and therefore perception and neighborhood and town to the state of relative innocence, utopian in hindsight—such purity, such sincerity—that had obtained before the advent of the corrupting love letters. Unfortunately, his ersatz correspondence, in the weeks that followed, achieved nothing so much as a refinement of the same locutions Mr. Brocklebank so hoped to be rid of.

He added: Marooned in the gallimaufry of these latter stages of corrosion, he could remember only that he wanted to be in some way other than he now found himself, unable to access words that might describe even to Brocklebank *sich selbst* what it was he might have lost.

Rumrill said: Reliant from then on upon Mrs. Brocklebank's reactions to his own assimilations of her usages to dictate his future practice and therefore thought and therefore behavior, Brocklebank must when his wife eventually vomited and dropped dead have felt positively orphaned. He had been robbed of the confirmation of himself as husband to a Mrs. Brocklebank; that is, a machine that recorded her numerous treasured fatuities, and so produced in Mr. Brocklebank's mind second- and third- and fourth-generation copies of her words and therefore actions, until the distortions soon overwhelmed the signal that had first set these echoes off.

He added: As parasites go, hostless.

Rumrill said: What was left of the unjealous urban Brocklebank was nothing much. A better solution was required.

He added: A widower's strategy.

Brocklebank writes: Fancying is that which creates me.

Rumrill said: On the subject of strategies, there was a month when I became convinced that the practical and palpable simultaneity of a mirror—as opposed to the simulated relationship between a live transmission or recording and its source—would be an effective means by which to defuse my phenomenological anxiety. I was able with the help of the hardware store in our town center, full of old-world charm, and now I fear defunct, to acquire a series of small square mirrors the size of my two hands placed side by side with their two thumbs folded under.

He added: And a hammer and some nails.

Rumrill said: After many a surreptitious appraisal of the suitability of my plan with regard to its placement along my favored route to and from the train station, I chose a sunny weekday morning to install my solution. I dressed warmly and left my home I think with a purposeful step.

He added: Earlier than usual, to give me time to finish the job before the library opened for the day.

Rumrill said: The idea was to provide myself a safe path at least as far as the station, upon which I would always be able to confirm easily the continued existence of my home. I would tack from mirror to mirror, a zigzag path, until I reached the train.

He added: In emulation of the same path taken by the reflected light coming from my home.

Rumrill said: The first four or five hundred yards were simple. I began with the siding of the house opposite mine, which splintered some under my hammer.

He added: But held the nail and the mirror.

Rumrill said: I moved to a nearby telephone pole whose placement was, is the term "kitty-corner," from the initial mirror. Such poles were indispensible to my plan, since these were placed along every street, evenly spaced one from another and of an ideal thickness, and curved too, which would allow the greatest possible flexibility in terms of angles of reflection.

He added: Or refraction?

Rumrill said: What I hadn't anticipated was that this work was noisy. It was a sunny and cold weekday morning and my neighbors and their neighbors weren't used to having their early hours disturbed by the sound of nails hammered through tin, glass, plastic, and wood.

He added: *Rumrill statant self-conscious gules.*

Rumrill said: Though "house-proud," let me confess that I was and am not what is called "handy." I found the job a little less simple in the commission than it had been in the conception.

He added: An imposter?

Rumrill said: It would however, despite my embarrassment, have been pleasant to my vanity to draw a crowd on that bright weekday morning. When I realized what a spectacle I'd made of myself, I was a little disappointed to see that my neighbors and their neighbors had weighed their options and decided that there was little profit in becoming involved in whatever had caused the noise that had disturbed their early hours.

He added: Also, I should have worn gloves.

Rumrill said: At best I proceeded by "trial and error." Something I had not anticipated was the great difficulty the vertical alignment of my mirrors posed.

He added: My inability to line them up correctly without a yardstick or some other tool or aid.

Rumrill said: I reached the train station, which was as far as my experiment could take me on that morning, to discover that, through the gradual, inevitable misalignment of my mirrors, the view I'd established, from my optimal vantage at the end of the mirror corridor—a squat of about four feet six inches below and to the right of the final mirror, located outside one of our neighborhood's much-mourned outdoor cafés—was mainly empty air and then a small portion of the lower left-hand quadrant of a second-floor window on the southeast façade of my house. I also discovered that I had been cheated of even the minimal comfort that I could probably have derived from this already unsatisfying view.

He added: Because the portion of the frame that did in fact contain a part of my house, and so might have served as proof of its continuance, was—thanks to a trick of optics that in retrospect I recognize was the only reasonable conclusion to my experiment—nothing more than a reflection of the view into a window of the house next door to mine.

Rumrill said: What I discovered was that the refractive index of my own window—unless I mean reflective—made it serve, when viewed from this angle in daylight hours, as yet another mirror, positioned in such a way as to provide a clear view into what I knew was one of my neighbors' bedrooms. For whatever reason—because it was in the shadow of my own building?—the window of my neighbor's bedroom was not itself reflective but perfectly transparent, though otherwise identical in every way to the glass of my own bedroom window, in size, shape, thickness, frame, the placement of its thin I think granite ledge, and so forth.

He added: Pigeons.

Rumrill said: Had this window in turn reflected my own window, my failure wouldn't have been quite so conclusive. Had this window in turn reflected my own window, I could at least have felt that the object of the experiment—palpable evidence of the continued existence of my home—had been attained.

He added: If not in the manner I'd foreseen.

Rumrill said: Had my neighbor's window reflected my own window in turn, I would at least have seen, in my nailed-up hand mirror, at the end of the corridor of reflections it initiated or concluded, a succession of windows, one of which, I could have told myself—in fact, I suppose, every second one—was my own. The appearance of this succession of windows in my nailed-up hand mirror would have acted as a guarantee that my house was, as we say, still a going concern.

He added: To be denied even this!

Brocklebank writes: The most diseased justification a cat fancier can give of his profession would be saying that it is somehow scientific.

Rumrill said: You will say that even the sight of my neighbor's window ought to have served, for me, as a guarantor of the continued existence of my home, since surely my own window would have needed to be extant in order to act as penultimate mirror in the corridor, and so reflect back the window I did not, nevertheless, want to see. To this I can only reply that such abstractions were of no use to me in the full flight of my phobia.

He added: *Any* edifice might well have borne a reflective surface at that height—as, indeed, could the cockpit of a helicopter, a curtain of especially refractive mist, or even a sheet of window glass peeled away in the wind from a nearby high-rise and en route to ground level to decapitate some accidental passersby.

Brocklebank writes: Holding at bay our awareness that we carry within us the chemicals cooked in the early earth.

Rumrill said: I then became preoccupied with the idea that I might utilize my mirror corridor, though a clear disappointment as a solution of the *Daseinstütze* type, for other purposes. Admittedly, to titillate oneself on a street corner on a weekday in the daylight hours is not a simple matter.

He added: But I considered myself a man of rare ingenuity.

Rumrill said: My neighbor at this time was not a comely young woman, as far as I was aware. I had not at this time seen any evidence of there being a comely young woman at residence in the building next door.

He added: But I could conceive of the possibility that one would eventually, in the near future, visit.

Rumrill said: This possibility seemed to me not unreasonable given the age of the neighbor in question, who had indisputably reached his majority and would soon naturally enough seek a wife with whom to share his worldly goods and in time produce off-spring who would perpetuate his modes of thought and behavior and make similar use of those words he had chosen in preference to others to describe our town and its numerous and pleasant attractions. It seemed entirely plausible to me that a comely inebri-ated young woman of the sort to frequent one of our drafty neighborhood bars would follow my neighbor, who was not an unpleasant man, or no more so than any of my neighbors at this time, back to his home, on our street, which in those days was rather quiet.

He added: Though not so quiet as now, I surmise.

Rumrill said: They would wake up late the next morning, because of their inebriation, too late for work, which they would skip, a sham excuse deliv-ered to their employers, first one and then the other, via telephone. I would have kept an unaccustomed watch of my neighbor's activities the night before and so would be prepared to call in my own sham excuse to my new supervisor at the library as necessary.

He added: What relief when I didn't show.

Rumrill said: I would then hike to the train sta-tion as though on my way to work in the morning on the sort of ordinary day the mirror solution had initially been conceived to improve. I would stop and assume the proper-altitude squat at the proper place on the street by the empty outdoor café and so see into some portion of my neighbor's bedroom, where a comely young woman was likely to be located.

He added: And so might stray into the frame.

Brocklebank writes: Only wanting to be friendly

to my colleagues, but they didn't want it, preferring to mock.

Rumrill said: Of course it hadn't escaped my notice that I would have a better and direct view into my neighbor's bedroom if I was stationed at my own bedroom window, which would certainly appear transparent from the inside of my home, if the sun was in the sky and my electric lights had been switched off. Our two windows were nearly parallel and I could easily crouch beneath or stand at an angle to mine and so have a comfortable view into a larger portion of my neighbor's bedroom, and thus increase the likelihood of said comely young woman's appearance.

He added: But this convenience was out of the question.

Rumrill said: My bedroom window had already been the subject of a previous solution to a previous problem, and to dismantle this relatively successful apparatus felt to me counterproductive. I had, you see, done everything I could to make certain that as little of what I might call the outside world was visible from inside my bedroom as could be managed without the employment of carpenters.

He added: Which would have aroused suspicion.

Rumrill said: I had purchased very thick drapes, which I still use today, and these were not only hung but taped to the wall around all of my bedroom windows. Though some light was let in, it was quite impossible to see any shapes through the stuff of those drapes, even if you stood very close and tried to peek through the weave.

He added: I speak from experience.

Rumrill said: When I was in bed at night, you see, I had suffered from what was perhaps the inverse, or do I mean obverse, of the problem I faced when I left my house in daytime. I couldn't fall asleep so long as there was any hint of evidence accessible to me in bed that my bedroom and thus house were in any way contiguous with and a part of the big world outside.

He added: Though I was greeted cordially enough at the grocery, in those days.

Rumrill said: I couldn't fall asleep so long as there was any sign present that my bedroom and thus house belonged to the environment that surrounded them, so long as I could not maintain the belief that my bedroom and thus house were somehow entirely different orders of space. I couldn't fall asleep with the thought in my mind that various rugged men and women had at one time in our town's prehistory traversed the open flatness of my neighborhood—their every sage pore cauterized by the sun's naked scrutiny—and judged it meet that all its blank space should be apportioned into cubes or other Platonic solids that would in time hold wood and stone and plastic in one or another style—or else, as you'll recall, the style of style-set-aside—in order to give the men and women who could afford this privilege a place to keep their belongings and beds and meager prospects for sleep.

He added: And the enjoyment of salacious thoughts as they try to drift off.

Rumrill said: It was impossible for me to sleep so long as there was some intrusion into my bedroom—in audiovisual form—of the notion that, in my bed, I was still outside, in what I refer to as "the big world," and in much the same way as I would have been on the way to or from the train station. It was a source of great anxiety to me, the prospect that there was no real *inside* to be found anywhere in the world, that all space is simply space, the same space, no different anywhere, save perhaps deep under the earth, beneath the flat plane that is our neighborhood.

He added: But think how difficult to dust your bedroom, down there.

Rumrill said: Not only would it have been laborious, then, for me to untape and then eventually retape my drapes so that I might better see my neighbor in the company of a comely young woman, ideally in a state of undress, this very procedure—and even were I rewarded with precisely the sight I had untaped my drapes to receive—would add another to the stockpile of thankfully distant, attenuated memories I had retained of the view outside that window in the days before it had been sealed: memories I'd hoped to leave unattended long enough that they would begin to pale further in the company of images newer and more colorful and of greater consolation. I mean of course memories that reinforced my sense of the fragility of the bogus "inside" to which myself and eventually my cats and before us in his wisdom Mr. Brocklebank all owe or owed the solidity of our daily activities.

He added: And by extension, sensations; and by extension, thoughts.

Rumrill said: It stands to reason, then, given my reluctance to untape my drapes, and so court a different sort of disaster than that which I feared as regards the disappearance of my home in the absence of my perception of it, that the only option available to me—if I wanted to look into my neighbor's window—would be to make use of those mirrors originally intended to maintain the consistency of a different, if nearby, location. Yet, were you the astute critics of my methods I'm sure I shall never have the pleasure to encounter, you would now be justified in saying that my mirror solution was actually a failure twice over.

He added: Once in that my own home was no more substantial now by means of the laboriously constructed corridor than it had been by means of my memory alone; twice in that another if nearby location and the likely or imagined events that might take place there, *so Gott will*, were now *more* substantial to me than my home, my dark bedroom, the slopes of gray, white, and black dust in its corners, my clammy and not-quite-made bed.

Brocklebank writes: Never aiming at an accord with the basic tendencies of our time.

Rumrill said: On the subject of comeliness, from which may we never be far, it stands to reason that the woman with whom I went on occasion into the stacks at the library was comely to an uncommon degree. I say this because the logic of my memories of the events she precipitated would demand that she be so.

He added: Though I've been wrong before.

Rumrill said: It stands to reason that I had some sort of sentimental rapport with the woman with whom I went into the stacks. I say this because the logic of human interaction insofar as it has been made plain to me indicates that a sentimental rapport would more often than not underlie such intimacy.

He added: Unless of course she'd mistaken me for someone else?

Rumrill said: There is also the possibility that, in the absence of a sentimental rapport, the woman in the stacks was simply the sort of woman in or out of library stacks for whom it was desirable to fuck men about whom she knew nothing and about whom she intended to learn little more than the fucking of such a man might teach. If so, then it would be unfair of me to say that what we might call our friendship was conducted without communication.

He added: Because what we did together in the stacks was itself our means of communication.

Rumrill said: It would be accurate to say that whatever acts in which I hoped my next-door neighbor and a comely young local woman might engage—with no reason to think themselves observed, in the comfort or in any event shelter of that bedroom parallel to my own—took the form, in my mind, of those same acts I remembered (clearly, in those days; the days, I mean, when I went around nailing mirrors to telephone poles) from my time spent with the woman with whom I went on occasion into the stacks. Or else, it would be accurate to say that when I try now, as an aged Rumrill, to picture to myself what I, as a young mirror-nailer, in front of a partially shattered and certainly warped hand mirror in full view of traffic on a sunny morning, hoped to see at the other end of his corridor of reflections, probably a mile or a mile and a quarter away, I am unable to populate that parallel bedroom—or parallel quarter-bedroom, since my view on the street by the outdoor café and the train station was hardly comprehensive—with any other series of actions aside from those that had been accomplished with my (by this time long since departed) female coworker.

He added: Presumably comely.

Rumrill said: As such, if I were to stand in full view of traffic on a sunny morning by one of our outdoor cafés, nearby both our grocery store and the electric rail station—all of which even at that hour would attract and disgorge their fair share of pedestrians—positioned at a telephone pole in a squat, the better to see down or into my mirror corridor, my behavior could therefore be characterized, precisely, as an attempt to "catch a glimpse," unseen, not of my neighbor but of myself and the woman in the stacks engaged in activities that I would not have cared at the time, while thus engaged, to be observed by any third parties, should such an option or threat have been presented. What had gone on in the stacks between my coworker and I apparently represented the limits of my conception of what my next-door neighbor and his comely local inamorata—or indeed the woman in the stacks and a Turkish soldier, for example—could show me.

He added: With carbon copies on pink onionskin.

Brocklebank writes: Someone always trying to get you away from the thing that you do.

Rumrill said: In the event, thanks to the sun

and the abundance of stimuli that susurrated at the corners of my eyes on the morning I constructed my mirror corridor, I was distracted from my thoughts of the likelihood of the appreciation of my neighbor and a local woman "pleasant to the eye" engaged in the selfsame acts that I and the woman with whom I went into the stacks had in bygone days pioneered, by the unfortunate intrusion of my own quarter-reflection several yards away, blackened and transparent in the café's window, mitigated by clouds, cars, and the criminal silhouettes of neighborhood passersby. In my eagerness to find a way to leave my home without the big world's misapprehension of this gesture as my tacit approval of its intent to submerge said home beneath whatever typhoon of the untenable would surely wash it out to sea from between the two more-or-less identical buildings on either side as soon as my back was turned, I had neglected to consider a related but till now essentially manageable subset of difficulties.

He added: What a pisser.

Rumrill said: I had, and at the least desirable moment, given myself accidental confirmation of *my own* substantiality via the practical and palpable simultaneity of this shop-window reflection: caught in the anticipation and even visualization of—at the other end of my mirror-corridor, in the quarter-bedroom of my neighbor—a reenactment of the well-worn memory of myself with my cock for instance in the mouth for instance of the woman with whom I had gone into the stacks. I could have turned my head back to avoid seeing myself if not in a grotesque leer then in any case guiltily receptive to the hoped-for sight of a man better able than I to persuade a comely young woman to accompany him back to his bedroom for the purpose of said reenactment for no known audience of what had once gone on in the stacks of our nearby public library, but the knowledge that this reflection was still there, visible, invariable, accessible to my eye, or indeed anyone's, accomplished for Rumrill himself the perfect, confirmable stability he so hoped, in those days, to achieve for his home.

He added: Through artificial means.

Rumrill said: While my home—which, at that moment, for all I knew, had been reduced by some cataclysm to nothing more than a single window suspended at second-story height in who-knows-what sort of viscous and uninhabitable ontological goo—remained elusive, despite its relative size, its motionlessness, indeed its thus far invariable persistence at the same address and in the same circumstances that I had first found it, I myself had become a certainty. No intangible perceiver, I found that I could be myself perceived while about the business of my degenerate perceptions—was myself a going concern in the big world's awful balance book.

He added: And this when I least wanted to be certain of myself.

Rumrill said: I don't mean to say that, previous to the sight of this reflection, this live portrait of myself as "dirty older man," I'd had the same phenomenological difficulty with regard to Rumrill himself as I did with Rumrill's home. Rumrill is not a shell or fur, and is not so easily shed as Rumrill's house.

He added: Difficult though it is to leave Rumrill's house.

Rumrill said: Curious to say, and though I have plenty of evidence in my files as to the changes Rumrill himself has undergone over the course of his life—typed and stored under a variety of headings in my many cabinets, for example: Shame, Illness, Dreams (Opera) and Dreams (Cross-dressing), Routes Through the Neighborhood, Thefts (Suffered) and Thefts (Perpetrated), Women Encountered, Conversations (Overheard) and Conversations (Imagined), Cats (Deceased) and Cats (Presumed Alive), Things I No Longer Remember, Spaces Through Which I Could Navigate Even Were I Blind, *usw.*—I still feel that I am in essence the same Rumrill as when I as a callow infant began this Rumrill business however many years ago. It may be that I discontinued the maintenance of my many records after so many years precisely because I began to see therein ample indications that I already bore little resemblance to the memory I still carried of the Rumrill as whom I began, despite the rigid regularity with which I thought my movements, and thus habits, and thus thoughts, and thus continuation, had been ordered.

He added: But who, if not Rumrill, could I be?

Brocklebank writes: All of us being bewitched, and mostly by accident.

Rumrill said: Given his own worries, wily Brocklebank, after his wife's death, in order to combat his own crisis of vocabulary and thus personality, decided to seek out or track down or look up or run to ground his wife's correspondent or lover or perhaps imaginary confidant. After all, he had seen the address on her letters, had he not?

He added: These records are hard to work with.

Rumrill said: So off Brocklebank went on his two legs to the house he thought might be the one to which his wife's letters were never sent. The house he identified from her half-remembered envelopes was distinguished from the others on its street in our neighborhood in that, while it had once been provided with a front lawn belonging in a general way to the *Poaceae* family, this had since been torn up.

He added: And replaced by gravel.

Rumrill said: Brocklebank knocked at a door he was not unconvinced would yield to him the sight when opened of the person his wife had likely been intimate with before her diagnosis. He was disappointed.

He added: The door neither opened nor made demands.

Rumrill said: As he would someday read was common practice in novels borrowed from the public library where once his dead wife might well have worked despite her age and illness—novels with many thousands of words pressed between their two covers devoted to descriptions of men who when confronted with unanswered doors try on manly whim to open them all the same, knobs or handles twisted with great force only to offer no resistance because left unlocked (the killer, sorry, has already made his getaway)—Brocklebank tried then on an irrational whim to open this door despite its reticence. The door, in turn—as it had read in novels wherein doors are confronted by impatient men possessed of manly whims and so creak in their hands ominously open—creaked then ominously open.

He added: Any objections?

Rumrill said: The space inside was dark. In the dark was an undistinguished man Brocklebank assumed must be he who had been so important to his late wife that she had never once mentioned him, the better to relish this secret association until such time when the ground of our quaint town would make unselfish room in its perpetuity to accommodate her bitter fats and marrow.

He added: I mean, if it was a he.

Rumrill said: When at last the figure replied to Brocklebank, it did not concede that there was anything out of the ordinary or even creepy about the presence of this very probably cuckolded and certainly unintived Austrian in its house. In fact, the figure spoke to Brocklebank as though Brocklebank had been expected, perhaps invited.

He added: Consternation.

Rumrill said: The figure would not even admit that Brocklebank was a stranger. The figure would not rise to shake Brocklebank's hand or to call the police.

He added: Unless I mean "nor."

Rumrill said: The figure in an accented voice addressed Brocklebank in such a wise: "You're late." Brocklebank, armed with only his own puny, now mostly flattened accent, found himself outmatched by a foreignness superior to his own.

He added: Outgunned and mute.

Rumrill said: In fact, the figure went so far as to admonish Brocklebank for his insensitivity. Had not he (Brocklebank) agreed to take care of his (we'll say) house and its many cats while he (this man) was out of town, and was he (Brocklebank) not supposed to have arrived to take up his duties days before this, and did he (B.) know how difficult, not to say expensive it would be for the man to replace his letters of transit, now voided—to find a new point of egress from our town?

He added: "You swine."

Rumrill said: When at last one malnourished cat of the supposed many behind the walls and under the floors made an appearance, its reaction to the presence of this not-yet-entirely-senile Austrian man was to attack him. Brocklebank for whatever reason felt smaller than this cat, which was no bigger after all than his dead wife's forearm.

He added: Minus hand.

Rumrill said: The man in the chair, who was not Brocklebank and who was perhaps blind or deaf or crazy or simply too polite to acknowledge Brocklebank as an intruder, gave his interlocutor neither satisfaction nor relief. The cat, however—if indeed it was a cat and not perhaps a dog or infant daughter or hapax legomenon, and whose attack drove Brocklebank out onto the gravel lawn—showed Brocklebank *some* courtesy in that it gave back to the widower in flight the proportions of a man with every right to exist in or out of the big world of our neighborhood and town or even as far away as Austria.

He added: By shedding his blood.

Rumrill said: The animal accompanied its victim home. That is, it hung from the torn skin on Brocklebank's arm.

He added: A little flag of war.

Rumrill said: In agony, unaccountably terrified, Brocklebank managed to get to his empty house and close and lock the very cooperative front door behind him. He squeezed the neck of the cat until it opened its jaw, after which, thrown to the floor, it was docile and even friendly.

He added: "Is this what they mean," wondered Brocklebank, "when they say 'it's better not to know'?"

Brocklebank writes: Knowing nevertheless that in the panorama of earthly things, cats are just one element of drama.

Rumrill said: Another example of a hard solution of the *Daseinstütze* type would be the hire of an individual to serve as caretaker whenever I could not help but leave my home. To hire someone as caretaker in my home would be, in essence, to hire someone to serve as a surrogate Rumrill.

He added: If only.

Rumrill said: However seductive this solution, it was too flawed to function. It could only be considered reasonable so long as we posit that there exists in the world a man or woman able to perceive my house and environs in the same ways, with the same attentiveness to which details, with the same inferences drawn, as I.

He added: Piffle.

Rumrill said: It isn't that I would accuse my hired surrogate of dishonesty, over the phone, when I would call him or her from whatever hideaway I'd found, whether abroad or in fact locally, the better to assess his or her behavior, and to reassure myself about the state of my home, its contents, its thereness there on the same street and at the same address, its number of windows and points of entrance, its eavestroughs, if that's the word. No, even a lie about my home might prove useful, in light of my disability, since a lie, however pernicious, would still imply that the site itself, at least, its substantiality, had maintained its continuity in my absence, even if subject to whatever disaster.

He added: Even if on fire, collapsed, flooded, sunk, ransacked, defaced, defiled.

Rumrill said: It comes down to a distrust of the terms available to my surrogate to communicate his belief that my house was in fact still a going concern, that nothing untoward—in whatever sense that Rumrill would find substantive—had occurred to my belongings or their respective places of rest. How could I trust that anyone else's definition of "fine" corresponds to my own?

He added: What a variety of propositional catastrophes might be hidden within or beneath the word "fine."

Rumrill said: But I came to the conclusion that to be informed over the phone or in a letter or even via signal mirror or flare by another human being that my house and its contents had not ceased to exist would be an ineffective palliative. It would have been impossible for me to visualize my surrogate in the transmission of his or her reassurances in the same space I'd hired him or her to oversee—via pen and ink or electronically diffused speech or flare gun—for if he or she were really able to stand in my accustomed place and see and report upon what I would myself have seen there, they would not be able to speak or write to me in their own voice and vocabulary and posture and preferences, but would have to make use of my own.

He added: Which is to say, Rumrill's.

Rumrill said: My absence and my surrogate's certainly alien behavior and by extension alien means of describing his or her temporary home to me over the phone or in a letter or with colored smoke would serve only to emphasize that while my house might not have disappeared in my absence, it had almost certainly become a *different* house. Insofar as my anxiety was concerned, to feel that my house had been replaced by an unfamiliar construction was in no way an improvement on the feeling that my house had ceased to be.

He added: Either way, out in the cold.

Rumrill said: This to discount the possibility that my surrogate, after all, would hope to disguise some actual indiscretion or error. This to take it as read for the sake of argument that my surrogate would only tell me the truth, insofar as he or she would be able to tell a truth of which this Rumrill could make sense.

He added: And that the house had not now been transplanted to where twin suns sink behind a lake, as strange moons circle, and black stars rise.

Rumrill said: I might after all find it crueler still to know that, rather than cease, my home and all my most dear and secret things, in their appointed places, had in the sight of a stranger been made into an unfamiliar territory stocked with artifacts indicative not of Rumrill but of an alien intelligence. Faced with this kind of invasion, if not subversion, of my space, I might even come to prefer the relatively innocuous threat of basic, if inexplicable, erasure.

He added: Curious to say.

Rumrill said: The open tap or electric lights or door,

on the other hand, though unable to hold up their end of a phone conversation, could be seen as facts, and like all facts would be able to communicate only one piece of information, in one single way—if mutely. The tap or lights or door could be relied upon to deliver the right message at all times without fear of interpretation.

He added: That is, their own continuity as facts.

Rumrill said: The problem, finally, with the tap or door or small controlled basement fire is that each of these solutions, more or less inanimate, more or less predictable, becomes, over time, less and less effective, more and more ignorable. They become, simply, part of the environment of the house.

He added: And so imperiled along with the rest of the scenery.

Brocklebank writes: Seeing myself as an adventurer, giving myself tasks without knowing how I am going to solve them.

Rumrill said: Oddly, whenever in those days I considered the possibility of a chance reunion with the woman in the stacks—and this independent of my hopes insofar as the goings-on in my neighbor's bedroom and my witness thereof through the mirror corridor, the details of these hopes freely adapted from my memory of the congruent goings-on between myself and the woman in the stacks back when I was employed at the library—or else, more precisely, contemplated the likelihood that I would, in reality, never again set eyes on that woman, which probability I rated at near certainty, I did not pursue this fiction to the extent of a recurrence or relapse between us of those activities the sight of which I now expected to see through the last or first of my cracked and partially untained mirrors. Instead, I pictured her and myself positioned at a certain intersection in my neighborhood, and Rumrill would say to her, "Here is a point I pass when on my way to the post office or the grocery; normally I turn left at this place, though I keep to the right side of the street; there is a ripped and weathered notice on that lamppost—hardly more than paper-pulp, rusted staples, and mildewed paste—which I've never seen whole, and so remain ignorant as to its intended message; yesterday, however, or perhaps last week, I altered my route, and did not pass here at all, for reasons that remain obscure to me, and yet, at more or less the same moment I would ordinarily have done so, I found myself looking, as it were, at the notice in my mind, and speculating as to what—if I can put it this way—it has wanted to tell me."

He added: And I picture her, if not interested, then listening with civil reserve.

Rumrill said: It could be that, even were the woman in the stacks and I to meet each other again, by chance, on a street in our town, which is easy enough for me to imagine, and indeed I have spent no little time on this pursuit—though it was beyond me then and is still beyond me to picture what she might look like aged through each day and minute that have followed her departure from the library and our town—she would not have the patience required to tolerate such an account of the true-to-life details of my walks to or from the post office or grocery. It could be that, even were the woman in the stacks and I to meet each other again by chance, she would not care to be reminded of the details of our friendship as it was staged in the stacks of our public library.

He added: Which scenarios—patience or im-, nostalgia or regret—represent, in all honesty, the full catalog of possibilities that I am able to anticipate.

Rumrill said: The precise circumstances of the woman in the stacks's departure from our town and the company of Rumrill remain opaque to me, I regret to report. Though I do know that the woman in the stacks took her leave before the inclement weather of whatever variety that made a great many of the older buildings in our town untenable.

He added: Even mushy.

Rumrill said: That is, the woman in the stacks took her leave—a turn of phrase whose provenance has always been a mystery to me—years before the time when your buildings, which still smell of wet, were erected, to the dismay of my neighbors and the frustration of many of my sovereign thoroughfares.

He added: "Time will easily scatter the tempest."

Rumrill said: I know that the woman in the stacks took her leave of Rumrill, library, and town before the rains because I now associate the memory of the probably marine twinkle through my bedroom windows, despite all my blinds and tape, with her absence. The light reflected by the river, for example, that perhaps took up residence on my street—over the inadequate drainage mouths clogged now with leaves and twigs and shoes and sediment and, for all I know, the stray cat who yowled periodically in the vicinity of my home in those days when there were no cats inside it to yowl back in sympathy or harmony or counterpoint—gave to my bedroom the feeling of a cabin on an empty seaside beach that one need never leave and of which one would never lose sight for miles in every direction, no matter how far one might walk.

He added: A moment of may I say reverie.

Brocklebank writes: Having the feeling some sort of black operation is about to take place.

Rumrill said: The solution I'd been in search of, the only feasible solution I've come up with—in any case the least flawed—was, in retrospect, as they say, "right in front of me." That is, I was blinded to the usefulness of this method by my proximity to it.

He added: Extant, available, fully formed.

Rumrill said: The solution I'd been in search of, in the abstract, was to install a self-regulatory network of independent perceptors to take my place on those occasions it was necessary for me to leave my home. The solution I'd been in search of was to install an autonomous intelligence that could resist being assimilated altogether into the landscape of my home, in my memory, just as the open tap, and other such devices, could not, thanks to a significant but above-all manageable degree of uncertainty in its behavior.

He added: As well as the necessity for *upkeep*.

Rumrill said: Unlike a caretaker, however loyal, honest, and true, the volatile but not significantly unpredictable intelligence that constituted my solution would be unable to make assumptions about or otherwise interpret its environment in a way that I would recognize as alien. My home would remain recognizably my own despite being perceived in its intimate details by a perceiver other than myself.

He added: Which is to say, Rumrill.

Rumrill said: I am not so naïve as to think that there is any intelligence in this world that does not as it were naturally and by reflex make assumptions about or otherwise interpret its environment. What concerns me is comprehensibility: so long as I could neither speculate as to the details of nor see such antinomy deliberately communicated to me by this other party, I would consider myself satisfied.

He added: "Ahead of the game."

Brocklebank writes: Excluding the gratification of physiological needs, physically harmful activities, and competitive activities.

Rumrill said: It must have been in that same bedroom, with that same incongruous maritime light upon my ceiling plaster, that I first really understood, as they say, "in my bones," that the woman with whom I'd gone into the stacks had left not only the library, where we'd met, but her neighborhood as well, which I'd never seen, and whose location I never learned. Given the totality of her absence, her nonattendance even at the inevitable chance encounters one is subjected to in our town's historic center, I have had to assume that she left not only her neighborhood but the town where we both lived, and in which, soon enough, would live a Mr. and Mrs. Pickles.

He added: And the country and continent and hemisphere as well.

Rumrill said: On my back, in my bed, with a river down my street, perhaps it occurred to me that if the woman with whom I'd gone into the stacks were indeed the sort of person to seek out encounters with strangers, much as she'd done with me at the library, then she might have left that part of the big world— with its stacks and library and train station and grocery—in the hope, exactly, of additional liaisons now in a timbre better suited to her adventurous tastes. A Rumrill, as her fellow countryman and townsperson, could not hope to provide the sort of experience she preferred.

He added: Which is to say, dangerous and dramatic, precarious and perilous, in diverse languages.

Rumrill said: Perhaps on a train en route to or from the sort of city a Rumrill would find exotic and difficult to imagine—let us say "Istanbul"—as she sits in her seat in her straight-backed and demur librarian's pose, with a book open on her lap in her native language—which she must still share, to her great dismay, with both Rumrill and the Pickles family—she would see, with or without his more or less well-behaved battalion, in their gray or brown and more or less well-starched uniforms, a soldier by an open window at the far end of her more or less well-maintained, if faded—could I say "wizened"?—and, as of now, sparsely occupied compartment. Perhaps after she sees him and he sees her, a signal will pass between soldier and librarian via a process of whose intricacies—so-called—I have only the vaguest grasp; and, though they cannot speak a word of each other's language, they will by means of a first gesture of complicity—the gift, I conjecture, unless one would say "loan," in one direction or the other, of a cigarette—soon find themselves between this car and the next, perilously engaged in acts similar to those in which I once partook, hidden from view by the Dewey decimal stacks at our town library, with this same woman in the middle of a different year, and in a different light, and at a different elevation relative to sea level.

He added: She conveniently in a dress.

Rumrill said: Perhaps while fucked by this starched soldier with or without a cigarette in his mouth—the familiarity and the ease with which she entered into this arrangement, I should say, seems to him a confirmation of various assumptions about her country and countrymen—the woman in the stacks on the train would see reflected in the semi-opaque glass of the adjacent car's door her enormous steamer trunk, shipped with her at no small expense across the ocean when she left behind library and stacks and Rumrill. Perhaps it occurs to the woman in the gap on the train that there behind her—though she can in this position "keep an eye on it"—her trunk is unprotected, and that, though too heavy to carry unaided, it could be easily forced open or tampered with while she is here immobilized.

He added: And yet, if we were to allow for the possibility of several conspirators in cooperation, the trunk might well be carted off on the backs of between two and four Turkish men, probably brothers, who would, later, with the trunk open in their home, the woman's many dresses and other accoutrements, equipment, impedimenta, and paraphernalia spilled onto their floor—those best able, I mean, to aid in the transmission of whatever *wortlos* information is necessary to encourage the approach of whatever men are most likely to fuck her in alleyways or on rooftops or between the cars of a train to or from the city we have designated, for convenience's sake, Istanbul—be themselves, I mean the whole family, confirmed in their various assumptions about the woman's country and countrymen, similar though not identical to those held by the solider who watches with interest as the woman's now somewhat older (it's been years since the library), could I say "wizened" rear end closes in repeatedly on what he knows must be, beneath his bunched shirttails and jacket, his bruised and now stinging accoutrements, equipment, impedimenta, or paraphernalia.

Rumrill said: In other words, supplementary to the wholly legitimate anxiety the woman in the stacks on the train might feel on her own account, in terms of her safety, at this Turkish moment—which anxiety does not worry her in itself, since it is part and parcel of the excitement she feels at the present moment, which after all she engineered—perhaps too she now experiences a certain trepidation (a twinge? a pit in her stomach? a shiver or chill, no doubt icy?) with regard to that enormous trunk which contains her belongings, each packed therein with great efficiency and an anatomical precision that will delight future archeologists of her country and countrymen when it is at last recovered, contents unusually intact, from beneath layers of oleaginous silt. Behind and likewise in front of her—in front of her in the reflection on the glass partition window—wedged into a luggage rack too small to accommodate it, which juts over her seat, vacated in order that she might join her soldier here in the loud and windy limbo between cars, to be suffused with the sensation of both panic and control that (probably) she so relishes, her gray or brown trunk bubbles in and out of a concavity in the semi-opaque shatterproof glass from which her face recedes and then approaches again as her soldier varies his hold on her and the tempo of his movements: her trunk, which, despite being portable, represents for her in her odyssey of anonymous sex with men who cannot speak her language a locus not dissimilar in its properties to Rumrill's house and cats.

He added: And so, profound.

Rumrill said: The woman in the stacks on the train is afraid for her trunk, but was not afraid for her trunk until she happened, just now, to see its reflection. This despite the knowledge that as long as she can see it in front of her—see the image that initiated her anxiety—it must be safe.

He added: Afraid for her trunk, afraid for her belongings, but afraid with a new sort of fear raised in particular by this visual confirmation—received by way of the semi-opaque, shatterproof, and now oily glass against which her forehead and cheek have been pushed—of the fact that there is, as yet, no need to be afraid.

Rumrill said: The woman in the stacks on the train could of course have changed her position to avoid the sight of the reflection of her trunk and the empty car around it and thereby remove the one irritant from this otherwise ideal (if that's the word) situation—said irritant now a sort of beachhead in her mind, within which conquered terrain the sensations and pleasurable-by-contrast anxieties she's traveled so many miles to indulge have been forcibly excluded—but this would mean the abandonment of the trunk to scenarios perhaps more dreadful still than those enumerated above, all of which were nonetheless imagined with her trunk's reflection's oscillations safely in her sight in the glass. That is, if the sight of the trunk's reflection had raised legitimate concerns— given that everything she's imagined to this point has been imagined with the ghost of her trunk kept at all times on view—to *not* see its reflection would make the trunk vulnerable to scenarios she couldn't even begin to imagine.

He added: Or at least not while fucked between the cars of a train to or from Istanbul.

Rumrill said: Further, the woman worries that if she should move her head or body or soldier in such a way so as to no longer be tormented by the reflection of her trunk and the empty car behind her, and likewise the now-baleful windows adjacent to her empty seat—which, from her angle of vision, seem to reflect in the shatterproof reflection ahead of her nothing more than the space corresponding to the lower-back of the passenger not yet seated directly below and to the left of her trunk—this might cause her, in time (contingent on how long she will be there between the cars, of course), to forget the threats to her trunk entirely. Though this would mean a relaxation of the fear that now causes her to tense her shoulder and stomach muscles in such a way as to make her position bent over in front of the door to the next car feel as awkward and uncomfortable as in fact it is, and though she would like nothing more, really, than to forget her trunk and apply her full cognitive powers to the matter at hand, the prospect of this possible future forgetfulness is cause for even greater alarm, which leads the woman in the stacks between the cars to recognize that, with regard to her trunk, there are not only first-order threats (for instance, theft) and second-order threats (without visual aide, and therefore without form), but also third-order threats, pertaining to fears that belong, properly speaking, to nightmare.

He added: For instance, that she had forgotten to bring the trunk in the first place (though what, then, had she been lugging from hotel to hotel?); that it's someone else's trunk, mistakenly brought aboard by a porter (if there are porters); that the contents of the trunk have been replaced by a bomb, or thirty-two piebald pigeons, or a chess-playing homunculus, or numerous rolls (reams?) of sandpaper, or the color red, or the smell of mildew, or a hapax legomenon, or Analytical Marxism.

Brocklebank writes: Making angular movements, almost like playing a pantomime; even trying to alter my handwriting to an angular, crabbed style.

Rumrill said: Don't think I haven't asked myself whether it might not be more plausible that the letters I discovered behind the green radiator in Brocklebank's guest bedroom were not in fact Mrs. Brocklebank's unsent correspondence to her putative lover, but Mr. Brocklebank's attempt to emulate

Mrs. Brocklebank's unsent correspondence the better to purify his mind and behavior of his self-inflicted infection with his wife's vocabulary. Which, if this is the case, must in turn mean that Mrs. Brocklebank had in the interim retrieved her original letters from their secondary hiding place behind the slumped but still sticky square of wallpaper in the foyer, which was printed with whatever sort of pattern would strike you as most likely—maybe prairie grass—and then destroyed or even mailed them off at last via the white van assigned to their part of our neighborhood, sent them off to the man or woman with whom she had or had not engaged in those activities Mr. Brocklebank had, rightly or wrongly, imagined.

He added: Surrounded by books on Byzantine architecture.

Rumrill said: This leaves open the question of how there could have been a single note, in that gorgeous hand, presumably from Mrs. Brocklebank's friend, unsigned, likewise in that parcel behind the green radiator in the guest bedroom, there to be found by myself years later along with Mr. Brocklebank's forgeries, if forgeries they were. I suppose that there is no more reason to assume that this document was itself the McCoy than were the letters signed in his wife's name by our own Mr. Brocklebank in his attempt to cleanse Mrs. Brocklebank's numerous treasured fatuities, devoid of any semantic import above that of a grunt or shrug, from his own interior phrasebook—such as, for instance, those *little hints* already mentioned, not to forget such chestnuts as "as such," and of course "of course," and indeed "indeed," and perhaps "perhaps," "part and parcel," "in fact," "might well be," and "by no means," and "so to speak," and "as it were," and "more or less," "and so on"...

He added: In their married decline reliant on imprecision to mask a not-infrequent confusion as to the mechanisms of causality.

Brocklebank writes: Cat-fancying might thus be thought of as the negation of simultaneity.

Rumrill said: Gruesome though his wife's death was, the manner of Brocklebank's demise ought I hope prove piquant enough to render that story insipid by contrast. For instance, why not, he sat without complaint in his favorite chair as his house burned down around him.

He added: Walls, hair, skin, facts.

Rumrill said: Sturdy men in fire-retardant uniforms stood in a circle by the flames of *Schloss* Brocklebank and called out to its owner that he must vacate the premises or meet an impressively grisly end. This while another group of sturdy men in similar uniforms presented an opposing view—and the first and larger assembly made no secret of their impatience with this splinter group—namely that the old man would have already succumbed and likely asphyxiated in the smoke produced by the destruction of all his plausible details a while ago now.

He added: And so was past rescue.

Rumrill said: In the meantime, I from my position outside the picture window saw with my two eyes through the glass Mr. Brocklebank inside his study, peacefully unconsumed in his favorite chair, a contented resident of this or that suburb of perdition.

My shouts or perhaps cries, possibly halfhearted, were ignored or remained unheard by the firefighters, who preferred to argue over the question of Brocklebank's decease than attend to the opinion of an amateur.

He added: A schism.

Rumrill said: I did my best to offer to both groups the gift of empirical evidence. They weren't interested.

He added: But, then, who is?

Rumrill said: Only later did I understand that the first (and substantially correct) group were in fact relieved to have this opportunity for debate, as they didn't want to be obliged to risk their lives to enter the house in order to effect a rescue. This while the second (heretical) group, for their part, were no less pleased to be engaged in argumentation rather than heroics, because they wanted nothing more than to see the first group proven negligent.

He added: The dangers of theory.

Rumrill said: Neither did Brocklebank himself hear my calls or pleas, deafened by the mastication of the flames or the hiss of his juices' evaporation or the screams of his thirty cats or absences of cats, which would I assume have been horrible to hear were their sounds not in turn overwhelmed by the voices of the firefighters' disputation or the aria of their siren. The floor-bound meteors that I saw hurtle past my vantage point—safe on the cool, wet stones of Brocklebank's front lawn—must have been those same unfortunate creatures whose status as animals alive or dead, actual or imagined, feline or otherwise, the flames conspired to keep concealed from Rumrill.

He added: One last time.

Rumrill said: In their furious movement I saw, as a cartographer might, the cats' varicolored perambulations, their sovereign thoroughfares through Brocklebank's house visible in the air, likewise on fire, soon a uniform orangey-red, which I think would be the proper hue under the circumstances. In the fire's consumption of these lanes and waystations I thought I could see, if for only a moment, and constrained of course by my dim conception of such, the lines and vertices of the great and probably useless contraption constructed by Brocklebank, now refined away in the heat until no more than its linkages remained: an indoor necropolis railway, independent of the spaces that had once contained it, lines in the air say upstairs or down, and imperishable.

He added: Uncorrupted by sense.

Rumrill said: What did not burn were Brocklebank's papers, his opus, his system, in conception, in utero, so diligently ruined by yours truly, the imp of unintended consequences; those papers that the old man had stored as though in anticipation of this holocaust in filing cabinets guaranteed by their manufacturer to be resistant to heat or wet. Skeptical though I was as to the veracity of this claim, in this case I must admit that my skepticism was unfounded.

He added: Another satisfied customer.

Rumrill said: Distracted from my fiery edification, I heard then that the schismatic firefighters had splintered yet again, which split resulted in the formation of a third and still more contentious group that had partially depleted the ranks of groups one and two. Faction three argued that there was no proof to be had that the owner of the burning house had been at home to begin with, and did this not better explain the occupant's apparent disinclination to be rescued from the fire?

He added: An open invitation to additional fringe theories.

Rumrill said: Factions one and two now saw themselves dwindled to a minority, indeed united in their obsolescence, as their ranks were again plundered by the naissance of a fourth group, who professed the most radical position yet expressed in today's synod. They claimed, not without vituperation, that Brocklebank had surely expired of causes *other* than those pursuant to the fire that had established so firm a foothold upon his goods and chattel, and that *this* scenario best explicated his silence in reply to their in any case halfhearted calls.

He added: Such as, "Hey, mister!"

Rumrill said: Would it come to fisticuffs, wondered Rumrill on the lawnless lawn. While Rumrill here and now wonders if there could there be a more beautiful sight in this lackluster world than men with the red highlights of an inferno on their lapels, ready to beat hell out of one another before a roiling conflagration.

He added: Blood in firelight is gray.

Rumrill said: Still, I was struck by the ingeniousness of their latest learned opinion. So much so, in fact, that I felt a sensation not unlike the one I experienced when first I found those letters secreted behind

Mrs. Brocklebank's radiator—now molten—or first heard or overheard the story of the mad mail carrier.

He added: That is: a sensation not unrelated to the mails.

Rumrill said: I felt as though I had been made privy to some exceptionally private disaster—I thought of the musty perfume of summertime underwear—with regard to which I would have done better to protect my naïveté, had I only known to avoid it. Which is to say that I felt discomfited, even guilty; I felt I ought to give up my attempts to attract the attention of the disputants.

He added: Rather than compromise myself.

Rumrill said: If Brocklebank had fallen prey to misadventure previous to the fire, then there could be only one person responsible, in his negligence, aside from the principal personage himself. What a short trip, then, from this realization to the inevitable accusation that would settle with Talmudic certainty upon the head of Reb Rumrill?

He added: Known as "The Exegete."

Rumrill said: After all, Brocklebank would not have been difficult to kill: he could not stand unaided, could not see the seams where what he might have forgotten had been elided from his life with safety scissors. Without such oversight, he tended inevitably—without the least need for encouragement on the part of his employee and sole heir—in the general direction of suicide.

He added: Or do I mean auto-chance-medley.

Rumrill said: In the same way that he would wash and rewash the same dish until his hands began to peel, he would, without supervision, inevitably take and retake the same pill until these made gobbledygook of his innards, each tablet to his mind the first of the day, and what a conscientious Brocklebank he was to have remembered to swallow it without Rumrill's prompts. On those occasions when Rumrillian vigilance did indeed lapse to the extent that a week's dose might be consumed over the course of a single afternoon, Brocklebank would thereafter cite the inexplicable depletion of his drug supply as evidence—during his next diatribe—that there were thieves to be found in every corner of this dishonest town; that his house was not secure; that his medicines were being pilfered and sold by myself to various neighborhood hooligans; that someone wanted to drive him mad.

He added: And absolutely mistaken about at least two of these points.

Rumrill said: The firemen's parliament had reached another impasse. It seemed there was now disagreement in the ranks of even the most radical splinter as to whether Brocklebank's pre-fire demise had itself *caused* the fire—for example a heart attack while at the gas range, or with match to cigar, or with armfuls of turpentined rags—or whether, instead, the fire might have been *engineered* in order to destroy whatever evidence the house might have contained as far as the real, foul-playful manner of the old man's dispatch.

He added: See the fingerprints sizzle off my favorite garrote.

Rumrill said: Cudgel them as I might, my brains refused to disclose any especially deadly liberty I might have taken, or neglect perpetrated, with or upon

Brocklebank's person or residence in the recent past. Nonetheless, this could hardly solace me under the circumstances; I could never be certain whether or not I had killed Brocklebank, in this scenario, since the old man had been a veritable encyclopedia of opportunities for murder, be it active or passive, violent or merciful, indeed undetectable, indeed inevitable.

He added: Or, anyway, manslaughter.

Rumrill said: To *not* have killed him would have been impossible to remember. As impossible in its way as not to remember no dream of Analytical Marxism.

He added: Inasmuch as I ever did or dreamed anything else.

Rumrill said: Could he while I helped him unmaliciously into his trousers one morning have been allowed to step on a tack whose microscopic colonists had fatally compromised his already feeble organism? Could I have introduced in my innocence a soupçon of rat poison instead of sugar substitute into his tea?

He added: Such similar bottles.

Rumrill said: These reveries, such as they were, were interrupted again by the voice of one of the fireman-disputants, who had now singled me out and summoned me into the circle at last. It seemed they wanted an impartial observer to hear their case and help them reach a conclusion without fisticuffs.

He added: Pity about the fisticuffs.

Rumrill said: I had wanted to escape the scene without notice. It didn't, however, surprise me that I had somehow made myself that much more notice-able a bystander by way of my guilty silence and decision to flee than through my *sogenannter* helpful cries and gesticulations.

He added: Typical.

Rumrill said: Two of the red men walked over to my station by the charred study's picture window and escorted me to the rocky front yard, where their comrades stood with friendly, professional smiles. As they collected me, they did not notice Brocklebank in his chair in the oven through the now-sooty glass.

He added: Though to say that one thing happened after another precisely is a misrepresentation.

Rumrill said: Surrounded now—my notes correspond with the minutes of the fire brigade on this score—I was made to listen a second time, at close quarters, to the several arguments still under consideration by these rubber-clad gentlemen, while behind and above and in front of us timbers cracked and crackled and carbonized and held their own disputations with the forces of gravity and chance in order to determine, and democratically, by which trajectory we bipeds below might best be squished beneath their magnanimous vegetable matters. By a curious effect of those natural laws that still do govern the travels of waves and particles and whatever other orders and principalities of pest unite in the frustration of our paltry attempts at communication in this town, I was less able to make out the firemen's words from my new position in their midst—such was the noise from the fire around us—than I had been back at my safer and certainly cozier locus, in attendance upon Brocklebank's slow roast.

He added: What a bunch of mumblers.

Rumrill said: From the proximity of their mouths and the wisps of benign gray curvilinear steam that burned off of their lips and beards, it was clear to me that, were circumstances different, and we had nonetheless made the unlikely decision to stand so close to one another, I should be not only irritated by their poor enunciation but aspersed with their spittle. Had I not been concerned that flight might incriminate myself further, there would have been little reason for me to endure their rudeness.

He added: Not to say vulgarity.

Rumrill said: "So you'd like to know," I asked them, "which of the scenarios you have formulated best explains why your ineffectual attempts to rescue the occupant or occupants of this house have till now proved unsuccessful? But have you not considered the possibility that the owner of the house might have moved away or indeed died and been buried or more appositely cremated months or years before the fire was started, and that what threatens now to flatten your pointed heads are the beams and timbers of a derelict edifice rather than a home owned or rented by a man possessed of a great many housecats?"

He added: Bigmouth.

Rumrill said: How, they wondered, could I—a bystander—know whether or not the house had once contained a great many housecats? How, they inquired, with the gestures and expressions familiar to me from past altercations with my fellow townspeople, best avoided, could I—whom they had never once seen at the grocery or post office or enjoying an iced coffee at one of our outdoor cafés or even spirituous liquors at one of our neighborhood bars—be so familiar with this their neighborhood as to know whether or not the owner or inhabitant of this house had once filled its every plausible corner with droves of good old *Felis catus*?

He added: Which is to say, *Felis catus domestica*.

Rumrill said: "An extrapolation," I mouthed bigly, "from the stench of this fire, which my rather sensitive nose tells me consists in its highlights not only of the smells of wood and gypsum being encouraged to part with those portions of their substance as might best be elevated into a gaseous state, but likewise that of fur, which is a zesty, even salty smell by contrast. For so much fur to burn along with the walls and carpets indicates to me—there is no mystery in it—that this must have been the residence of a great many housecats; if not now, then in the building's recent history."

He added: Vacuum as one may.

Rumrill said: They seemed little reassured by my explanation, perhaps resentful that they had themselves long been without functional senses of smell, and asked how I could be so certain that this fur was feline, that it had not perhaps been shed by *Canis lupus familiaris*, or—why not—*Atelerix albiventris* for that matter? Was I not mistaken, or overconfident in my ability to differentiate one type of burned filament from another?

He added: Marmot from flax, for example?

Rumrill said: "Why not ask," I asked, "whether or not we are even in conversation here, given the odds against such a thing, particularly by the light of a house on fire, whether or not inhabited by a great many housecats, and most particularly given the probable differences—in class, upbringing, education—between yourselves and this citizen, which is to say Rumrill, so eager to be of help? Why not ask," I asked on, "whether or not we could hope to understand a word of what we would be likely to say to one another, if this conversation were indeed to take place, given not only the noise made by said house on fire, catless or catful, but our incompatible vocabularies, due again to the aforesaid differences in class, et cetera?"

He added: Which just made them angry.

Rumrill said: Better still, they asked sarcastically, why assume you are anywhere but in your foyer, in conversation not with us but with guests intent on a tour of your own cat-infested home, but kept as it were in limbo by your interminable garrulity, no doubt of sinister purpose? Why assume our conversation is anything but a conversation related at second hand in the context of a still longer and even less likely conversation between people of unequal social standings, intentions, desires, possessions?

He added: The hell you say.

Rumrill said: Better still, they averred, hostile to me it now seemed, their eyes reservoirs of sooty pigment ready for the stylus, why assume you are anywhere but at your desk, at your typewriter, on the inside of a still-unblackened picture window, your attention taken at this moment or the next by the pitted street beyond, your rounded back pointed at the little world of your home behind you, preparing the script you will read when in time your guests knock or ring at your door and you invite them into your vestibule from which even they for all their boorishness will be powerless to escape, thanks to etiquette and self-interest? Why assume you are surrounded by malnourished men with the faces of prisoners possessed of neither the desire nor the incentive to fight a fire set on valueless property when it is far more likely that if you should turn your head in a moment of doubt over the use of the word "averred," you would find yourself hemmed in not by your fellow citizens but by filing cabinets stuffed with numerous variations upon the same hypotheses we are now compelled to mouth at your insistence?

He added: Impressive stuff, without benefit of saliva, given the heat.

Rumrill said: "Better still," I countered, "why assume our conversation is not in fact a garbled *third*-hand recitation from the spotty notes taken by those supposed guests of mine to their own guests in turn, after many years, when one or the other has likely died of whatever disease it is our town water supply seems to encourage; notes supplemented by whatever other documents might have survived into that distant day, filled with errors and misunderstandings, we cannot doubt, all of which would certainly explain the manner in which we seem to have been condemned to express ourselves on this unseasonal day? Why assume that what we've experienced and said to one another is anything but some archivist's fantasy, a mistaken correlation made between two different events that in reality occurred on different days, even in different years, recorded poorly by the poor historians of our town, forced to rely on accounts badly distorted by their own inattention as well as various natural disasters?"

He added: Floods candy all sins over.

Rumrill said: "Better still by far," I suggested, "why not presume we are all asleep, and that this situation is—by way of one of those simplistic inversions typically mistaken for wit—a dream, or else, why not, that we have been gang-pressed into someone else's dream, indeed the dream of a man who, his employer dead on account of causes either natural or otherwise, and himself therefore the inheritor of a great many unwanted housecats, has planned to set fire to the old man's house, the better to rid himself of this burden—which, heaven knows, the humane society didn't want to hear about—and then, after one too many marzipan balls before bed, is nettled through the night by dreams as to the possible ramifications of this act, legally as well as morally? Indeed, why not presume we are all the dream of one of the old man's unfortunate cats, who, having overheard the arsonist-hopeful's muttered debate on the subject—because he has already taken up the old man's habit of vocalized self-address as he goes about his daily rounds—is now curled fretfully by a heating vent listening to this ludicrous though ominous scene but no more able to make anything of the noises that come out of our throats than we might its mewing beneath the skirt of an ottoman?"

He added: Or do I mean tuffet.

Rumrill said: Not a little proud of this unexpected prolixity in the face of the fireman-synod's metaphysical antagonism, I was quickly reminded by their expressions that my waggishness was entirely lost on such men—even more so, I suspect, than it is lost on you. They looked if anything grimmer than ever, unless this darker hue was the result of the now setting sun's duet with the dust and light thrown up by the fire.

He added: A jury of my peers.

Brocklebank writes: Dealing with time inside their homes, fanciers mostly work with a linear idea of time, a "quantity" of time, and with time as a vectorial element, treating it just as a "white" component both of the structures and the experiences derived from those structures.

Rumrill said: What might be gained, I hypothesized, some time later, in my new house, with my new furniture, with my new income, and given my situation, my condition, my environment, if I were to abandon all of my other solutions, be they hard or soft, to follow my late employer's example, and rather than the construction of yet another and more complicated mirror corridor, for example—at which endeavor I might well fail due to my natural inaptitude—and in the absence of any great inspiration as to the construction of some new device whose many gears and arms in movement might when I am away convince me of the perpetuity of my home, what might be gained, I speculated, if instead of whatever best-laid plans, I acquired for myself a great number of housecats . . . would these animals not serve as the discrete perceptors I hoped would anchor my plausible home in place, and so provide the security I required to stray as far from this site as circumstance or whim might dictate? Was this not, perhaps, the same reason Brocklebank himself had invited into his home a mass of reliably inscrutable, contradictory, heretical points of view, to form in aggregate a process into which the gradual disintegration of his memories and thus habits and thus identity could be subsumed, and so convince himself—even when there was no longer a himself, properly speaking, to convince—that he still existed?

He added: Not unlikely.

Rumrill said: Perhaps in homage to his testament, whose pages by and large remained intact, or as intact as fire and flood and forgetfulness and sabotage were likely to leave them—albeit without any consultation of Brocklebank's precepts, or do I mean prescriptions, which I found and find impenetrable, and which he and I in any case rendered nonsensical through illness and indolence, respectively—I built for myself out of the warm parts of however many cats a machine, a perpetual-motion machine, if you like (if I may describe the activity of perception, tell me what you think, as motion; and if I may describe perception, likewise, as an activity). I made use of Brocklebank's example rather than what remained of his opus after its destruction or rather near-complete erasure at the hands, so to call them, of his disease, and then, with a greater degree of accuracy, of one Mr. Rumrill, given that I was at birth gifted with at least a couple of these useful implements—I mean hands—I made use that is of my memory of his disintegrated memory, substantiated of course by the endless supply of charred potshards left over from my late employer's oeuvre, to build my own system, which would, with minimal maintenance, operate independently of my perception, to ensure the continuity of the said Mr. Rumrill and his home.

He added: Which is to say, Rumrill's.

Brocklebank writes: We are just now remembering how long a well-run household can last and only now becoming civilized enough again that we want to fancy cats continuously.

Rumrill said: My machine, if you will, allowed me for a time an unprecedented freedom of movement, until, by and by, as I walked with elegance my sovereign thoroughfares through this our town, I came to two conclusions on the same wet day. I will note for your appreciation that this day was more than adequately lit.

He added: From above.

Rumrill said: For one, the more I walked secure in the certainty of my home's solidity as ensured by its twenty independent perceptors, the less I was able, in the placement of one facile foot after the other upon the neighborhood earth or concrete or tarmacadam—both singular and plural, as is its right—to see the town around me, and its halibut-men likewise, as anything other than a semi-opaque setting for the jewel of *Schloss* Rumrill. That is, the substantiality of my home in the absence of my firsthand and eloquent apprehension of its many qualities now *overwhelmed* the bland and by contrast attenuated ontological substance of the streets and lawns and crumbly ochre multi-story terrariums that make up the salient architectural characteristics of our town, long past its prime.

He added: Where once was assembled by sturdy men with pipefitter's cocks the noble Pullman car.

Rumrill said: I mean to say that my home even in my absence had now become a sore of sorts in the septic mouth of our town, worried at incessantly by Rumrill, try as he might to leave off. The tongue in this analogy is perhaps his body, muffled in wool; or else, muffled in wool, his mind.

He added: Such as it is.

Rumrill said: What use, then, my feline improvement upon the slapstick of the mirror solution if the treatment for my condition had drained the vitality from the big world I'd sought so long to enjoy without fear—had made it into as insipid a soup of compressed and attenuated images as my home had once threatened to become without my presence to shore up its lines and angles and spiders? What use, then, to undertake a morning constitutional to places I had hoped to see at last unplagued by anxiety over my base of operations when whatever scene the big world presented for the delectation of Rumrill would be invaded at all times by the relentless gray gravure formed by those twenty independent perceptors back at home, their little muscles, bones, and brains worked with patient application over every friable surface in said base.

He added: Every doubt pounced upon, toyed with, then devoured.

Rumrill said: Which line of thought led me to my second conclusion, namely that if *Schloss* Rumrill had previously been rendered unstable in my mind by the absence of a Rumrill within its perimeter, or in any case close enough to see it with or without the aid of lenses or mirrors or accomplices, the same, I now realized, had never been true of the big world outside its walls. If anything, there, the opposite or obverse obtained; stern measures were necessary to *forget* the big world even for a moment, and if to my relief I had on occasion been able to dismiss or set aside the threat outside my walls, for example when asleep, I had never once—pleasant though I would have found this reversal—been in a position of doubt with regard to the essential endurance of this our town's lanes and parks and bars and comely or otherwise citizens.

He added: Despite its or their invisibility and for preference inaudibility to Rumrill in his comfortable redoubt.

Rumrill said: Here, I realized, with no small distaste, was an object—I mean the big world itself, complex though it is, and populated with all manner of sub-object: so many nooks, compartments, sections, and appendices, at all points of the day or night, the sun or not-sun shining as is their preference over our flat and pitted plains as well as the minarets or do I mean spinets of Istanbul, property in either case of the Turks; and despite my inability, indeed disinclination, to perceive it in whole or even, fully, in part—that persisted in being, will I or nil I, *ever present.* The big world, I mean, was everything I had always wanted my home to be.

He added: Even possessed, I did not doubt, of nicer sofas.

Rumrill said: And the big world had never needed cats or mirrors, though in its diabolical excess it produced these in numbers with which *Schloss* Rumrill could never hope to compete. The big world had a functionally inexhaustible supply of eyes and ears and noses all screwed into the proper sockets in the monstrous machine of its perpetuity, all at work despite themselves to keep itself extant, insensible of the loss should Rumrill and his meager by contrast and singular by necessity perceptions and thoughts and preferences be put paid to by the agents, without number, the big world might, in its great malice, send after him.

He added: Alone or in force.

Rumrill said: If the big world outside the walls of my home was a far more reliable domicile for Rumrill than however plausible and well-adapted a shelter he had established for his sofas and boot-checks and umbrellas, what then did this mean for such a struc-ture—ignored—and such a man—alone? If his home and self and furniture—this latest set recovered by and large from a demolished hotel, not to mention those pieces salvaged from Brocklebank's house—were no more substantial by comparison with the big world around them than would be the libretto of an opera dreamed and enjoyed and then forgotten com-pared with the works of the Second Viennese School, what had I or Brocklebank before me accomplished with our cats save pervert with our own pettiness that greatest and most reliable system of all, which had our entire lives sheltered us without our knowledge from whatever greater oblivion seethed beyond its borders?

He added: For shame.

Rumrill said: In sum, the big world was always there, is always there; whereas my little world, and my little self, are not, cannot be. Cats or no cats, I cannot aspire to real solidity.

He added: Where am I, do you think, when the world can't see me?

Rumrill said: And I am no more convinced of the viability of a Mr. and Mrs. Pickles, or even the latter's childish underwear—decorated in what I will call bad faith with crude red images of strawberries no doubt reproduced thereupon by a machine that followed with the best of intentions the design of a man or woman with no love for the fruit in question—and likewise the humid apparatus, as I am pleased to call it, its taste not half so harmless, now sheltered beneath, than I am of a Rumrill or his thoughts or shoes. When I can't see or imagine you, when you can't see or imagine me, we all of us recede not into the nothingness I had so feared, but into the big world's *liquor amnii*.

He added: The tides of unlikelihood.

Brocklebank writes: No one really knowing what the quality of being human actually is.

Rumrill said: Little though I appreciated my role as one among millions or billions of anonymous, unseen, ontologically unstable but nonetheless discrete preceptors whose function in aggregate was to keep the big world from the big nothing behind or beyond its shores—as opposed to the little nothing to which the inattention of a Rumrill temporarily consigns whatever object or individual, be it dear and secret or otherwise—I could not ignore the fact that with my home now safe in a secure and stable state, fixed in position even when my back was turned, a Rumrill at large, anxiety free, tied to such an anchor, served only to further sap the substance of our already faded town. I had in my desire to walk our streets free from apprehension done little more than upset one subsystem of the many upon which the big world's constancy is founded.

He added: Rumrill the poison in the well.

Rumrill said: Not that the big world cares any more when this or that island of sense is submerged at a given moment than I did or do when a particular cat from my menagerie—or Brocklebank's before me—takes a momentary powder. We each of us, as units, are expendable.

He added: Our opinions, sensations, itches, and ingenuities all irrelevant.

Rumrill said: But the ramifications of my subversion, intended to be not momentary but lasting, extended farther than my own disappointment, difficult though this was for me to admit. If one little space inside the big world could be made, after all, to compete in its little way with the solidity of the big world around it—and even if all space is the same space, only apportioned by our human hubris into shapes of whatever size—then would this victory not upset, however subtly, the larger system inside of which the little world and its constituents were meant to function?

He added: Substantiality a resource apparently in finite supply?

Rumrill said: I had found a way out of one trap

and into another and more dangerous one. I felt, more and more, that I could neither stay home nor go out—could neither dismantle my own system and so abandon my life to mere ghostliness, nor walk the streets "backed" by my cats and so watch the big world slide along with this and every Rumrill into the pit.

He added: A very practical, if inconvenient, afterlife.

Rumrill said: For if our town, which Brocklebank mistook for a prison, had been engineered—had been filled with people just as my house had been filled with cats, to keep the little or big void away, in the town's case, from the dry plains that surround it—what did my success as far as my phobia mean for those people, their fates, their sovereign thoroughfares, their under ordinary circumstances insignificant portion of the world machine for which they'd been designed? What, then, did my success imply for our town as far as our nation, our nation for our continent, our continent for our hemisphere, our hemisphere for our world, and our world for the something outside of our world, still so desperate not to disappear after however many eons of tedium?

He added: *Exhilarating Science-Fiction Tales.*

Brocklebank writes: My *Nutrition 1960 No. 5* concerning a butterfly or any number of butterflies turned loose in the habitation area.

Rumrill said: As to dreamed operas, there was in fact no third act to the one I've mentioned, in case you need closure on this point. Unless of course the scenario that followed it was in fact the third act, in some manner I can't recall.

He added: Or don't understand.

Rumrill said: I left the auditorium and continued to the train station in our town center after the conclusion of the aforementioned performance to catch the train that would take me home. As we rode underground toward the Shrieking Bridge, I realized by way of his reflection in the window across the aisle that in the seat next to me, stooped, was dead Brocklebank, bulge and all.

He added: Alive and along for the ride.

Rumrill said: When at last we emerged into the daylight it was not to cross the Shrieking Bridge and then return to the depths, as is the usual route, but in fact, and contrary to the course of the tracks as I knew them, to leave our town entirely, which I guessed must be somewhere behind us, at the other end of a tunnel whose darkness was, to my eyes, absolute.

He added: Because no light had been dreamed there.

Rumrill said: I felt at first an inexpressible and likewise inexplicable relief at the sight of the intermittently green if not exactly verdant, indeed somewhat blasted terrain beyond the bounds of our town, which—used as I was to our strict and depopulated horizon—almost boggled the mind with its admittedly very slight inclines and hillocks. I could not and cannot remember the last time I would have seen the land outside our town from such a position, save perhaps when first sent there by I believe my parents.

He added: Or warders.

Rumrill said: With the sun on our faces I looked around at the other passengers. Their faces were the faces of people I suppose I had seen in life on the train on my morning commute.

He added: Extras.

Rumrill said: I felt the good realistic throb of train-wheels as they passed over metal seams. A woman two rows behind me was deeply involved in her magazine and its vivid colors, a ready anesthetic for what I supposed must be a lifelong regimen of puzzlement and anxiety.

He added: And I breathed believable conditioned air.

Rumrill said: Peculiarly, and as would be natural I suppose on a proper transcontinental train—but would be quite unusual, under ordinary circumstances, on a small, electric commuter line—there was a sign above the doorway to the next car that sought to inform all of us unreal passengers that the club car was two sections on. As I was thirsty—or so my dream decreed I be; what I experienced physiologically I couldn't say—I stood and advanced through the aisle.

He added: Toes tread upon all the way.

Rumrill said: I pushed on a panel in the door stamped with just that verb; it slid open and I was ruffled by prairie air and the now un-muted train sounds, which were loud and improper to our timid commuter rail. I crossed between the cars, this space happily free of any assignations in progress, only to find, in the next car, familiar heads, noses tapered toward the door on the opposite end of the car.

230

He added: Consternation.

Rumrill said: I noted with alarm the same magazine-reader, and then, two rows farther, another Rumrill and Brocklebank, each as badly postured in their seats, bored and thirsty and none the wiser. To my dismay, this new Rumrill swiveled around and spotted me almost at once, and his shock was horrible to see as I-me rushed back toward my car of origin to find it just as I'd left it.

He added: Shy a Rumrill, but otherwise identical to the next car.

Rumrill said: Rumrill-two, now behind me, demanded to know had happened. I could only shrug and hold tight to the thin lizardy lips of the doorjamb.

He added: If they are called jambs on trains.

Rumrill said: When Rumrill-two saw my car, he sagged in his shabby beige suit and stared up at me (he was a little shorter) with eyes mostly white and terrified. Now *his* Brocklebank had lifted his shaky head to watch us, twisted in his seat.

He added: Unnerved, but less so.

Rumrill said: Decisive action was called for, I decided, and so shoved my shorter counterpart out of the way (I did feel a certain distaste for the fellow). My majestic stride covered his duplicate car in three giant steps, after which I opened the next door.

He added: To release another draft and din.

Rumrill said: Again I saw my car replicated, once I'd crossed through the wind and noise: Rumrill-three and his Brocklebank, without a care. This Rumrill, in gray gabardine, had just now decided to find the club car, forever two compartments ahead. Fascinated, I watched him exit at the next door ahead and then fly back in after a beat, panicked; we made eye contact just as Rumrill-two caught up, behind me.

He added: Out of breath.

Rumrill said: We three Rumrills stood locked in what I suppose would be called a deadly stare, until, just like that, Rumrill-three fainted dead away. With impossible vivacity, his own Brocklebank was on top of him in a jiffy.

He added: An attempt at mouth to mouth.

Rumrill said: "What is to be done?" asked Rumrill-two, now limpeted onto my sport coat. I shed it with another shrug on manly whim and moved on without reply, intent on seeing the next car down: my fourth.

He added: And hopped over my own unconscious body on the way.

Rumrill said: Lo, past the same wind and rumpus between the cars, I found another carbon copy—with a Rumrill who snored like a concierge and a Brocklebank with his hands on his window, eager to take in the unremarkable landscape that unspooled as backdrop to this vaudeville. Shortly after, Rumrill-two arrived on the scene, my abandoned jacket folded tenderly on his arm.

He added: What a sweetheart.

Rumrill said: He tried to take my hand. Again I ditched him to check on the next compartment—who knows what I hoped to find—but I was forced into a retreat when the door ahead opened all on its own.

He added: Or rather, on account of Rumrill-five or twelve or twenty-nine.

Rumrill said: In he staggered in a tuxedo, torn at the shoulder, and his face bore a week's worth of stubble. I must have made a sound, in shock, for Rumrill-four woke up.

He added: With a start.

Rumrill said: The newest arrival, so smartly dressed, staggered toward me and fell. I caught him, and he weighed almost nothing.

He added: As most things do, or rather don't, in dreams.

Rumrill said: "There's no food, no water!" sobbed this Rumrill. "No conductor, no engine!"

He added: "Only car after car of Rumrill after Rumrill!"

Rumrill said: When I was able to speak, I found that an evil thought had filtered up from my guts, and I presented it to the assembly. My dream had dictated to me what I needed to say.

He added: And I was, for once, word-perfect.

Rumrill said: "One of us has passed out in the car behind us," I said. "Lot of meat on him," Rumrill-two added, and he drew an hourglass figure in the air with both his hands.

He added: Which was followed by a novelistic silence.

Rumrill said: This was in turn followed in not much time by mournful nods, even from one or two Brocklebanks, for we were determined to survive, and food was the first order of business. We steeled ourselves and headed back through the rows of reproachful passenger statuary, and—lucky thing—I woke up.

He added: Before I was forced to taste my own tongue.

Brocklebank writes: A system implying violence, even vandalism, and, as such, disturbing.

Rumrill said: Another crisis soon compounded my recognition of the big world's superior reality. Do you remember, who knows many hours ago it was, when I told you that after several years of life here alone in this house, purchased with my Brocklebank-gotten gains and in no time filled as perhaps he would be happy to hear with the stable quantity of animals I habitually call "my cats"—though certainly many have died and been replaced through the good offices of, initially, the local animal shelter, and then my own skill as harvester of the population of animals abandoned on the streets of our neighborhood; and though just as certainly I am hardly prejudiced against non-feline animals, when, "in a pinch," it is necessary to substitute mammals of some other order to take the place of one of my twenty cats—that I gave up my records as to Rumrill's activities, gave up the use of those filing cabinets in a room no more than twenty brisk paces from where we now stand so pleasantly out of the storm?

He added: Or sun.

Rumrill said: The real reason for this was that after several years of life alone in *this* house with my twenty cats, which themselves followed other years of Rumrillian life in other places, though places not far distant—for instance the loathsome apartment house I had so desired to keep present in my mind while away the short distance to the train station or grocery—I decided under the influence of who knows what unclean spirit to review some of my older notes, "for fun." When I did so, I began to see what I considered worrisome patterns.

He added: Worrisome because, till then, invisible.

Rumrill said: Rumrill recorded, on June the fifth, in the file consecrated to his expeditions outside of his house, the necessity for such a venture on June the sixth, through the streets, sodden in summer, unless it was then parched, by way of one of his sovereign thoroughfares to purchase what the grocer was pleased to call farm-fresh eggs—though it's difficult for me to believe that there were, even then, any farms in the vicinity of our town, which fact made those words into another phrase whose provenance is lost to us yet which we cannot help but reiterate or perhaps regurgitate in our ignorance. (Which phenomenon will no doubt continue until the day when at last it is given for us to cease these imitations of our fellow animals still at motion and still at pains to make themselves understood but instead our fellow animals now within or distributed upon the body of the earth as parcels of agreeably inanimate humus.)

He added: (Amen.)

Rumrill said: Rumrill recorded, regardless, that such an expedition was necessary because there was no food in his house and because the grocery had recently issued a ukase to the effect that no further delivery boys would be wasted on so unreliable and argumentative a client. No further delivery boys of either gender would be sent to squander their hours in dispute with a crank who could no more remember the price of a carton of farm-fresh eggs than the basic courtesies due men and women in the service industry.

He added: Perhaps under the misapprehension that I was still Brocklebank's assistant.

Rumrill said: In the file consecrated, on the other hand, to Shame, I found recorded an entry identical to the one made on June the fifth with regard to June the sixth, made in this case on June the eighth with regard to June the ninth. That is to say, I found evidence that Rumrill must have consumed a dozen eggs in the brief interval that stood between the one expedition, presumably accomplished on the sixth, and the next, planned for the ninth.

He added: When I had no memory of even a single omelet.

Rumrill said: This peculiarity led me to examine several files in parallel, in search of other redundancies or contradictions. This peculiarity led me to wonder whether it might not be possible that someone had falsified or disordered my records while I was out of the house on an errand.

He added: But who, and why?

Rumrill said: When I went back through those details of my life I had considered worthy of rescue, of preservation in Brocklebank's blackened and scarred but nonetheless intact filing cabinets, which I had rescued from the railway graveyard where they and other of Brocklebank's belongings had been dumped, perhaps "unceremonially," by the authorities, I was alarmed to discover greater incongruities still. Conversations

(Overheard) would report for instance that I had eavesdropped upon a young married couple along my walk to the post office as they sniped at one another over their frustration with their narrow and damp apartment, and indeed their financial troubles, and how they would hardly turn their noses up at a little extra income, no matter how menial the work to earn it; while Things I Have Forgotten would report the same encounter, at the same intersection—down which ran one of my sovereign thoroughfares—and would employ the same phrases, exactly the same commonplaces, for example "turn their noses up," albeit with regard to another day entirely.

He added: With carbon copies on pink onionskin.

Rumrill said: I began with no little trepidation to face the likelihood that there was a force at work here that I did not understand; that despite the fact that I had acted, for Brocklebank, toward the end of his life, as the instrument or accomplice of his disease, that his system, as intended—whatever it was he had intended, whatever message his complete works might have held for its ideal cryptographer had it been completed to Brocklebank's specifications without its degradation by the nonsense signal of his disease, and then of course by yours truly, in the role, mustachios a-twirl, of our landlord Mr. Entropy— might nonetheless have *survived through me*, the agent of confusion, ridicule, slapstick. Was it not possible that, despite the incoherence I'd introduced or midwifed into his work, I was no longer in the world as I remembered it, but in the world-plus-Brocklebank's-system?

He added: And hadn't even noticed the change?

Rumrill said: Could it be that my place, as I saw it, in the by-comparison open-ended, emancipative equation posited by Rumrill to allow him the freedom of our stagnant town, unsettling as its ramifications had proven, was only an insignificant line in a far subtler program? Could it be that the holes I'd already found in my own so-called system, in my mind, in the sequence of Rumrillian events, all of which had seemed to me so orderly in their initial years, were in fact lacunae opened with intent by a force whose objectives ran directly counter to my own—an infection that had been nurtured through its infancy by Rumrill and his house and his cats?

He added: And had now filtered even into the big world around them?

Rumrill said: Could it be that Brocklebank's system had sought from its conception not to order a new manner of thought, as he had claimed, and not to quiet the anxieties of a solipsist, as I had in turn expected, but instead precisely to undermine the systems already in place to keep our town and the big world around it from an insubstantiality more dreadful than that which I'd feared would consume my home and biscuit tins whenever I went to work? Had Brocklebank, unable to escape the prison camp for which he'd mistaken our town, left behind him the materials for a bomb that would bring down the walls of this prison and all other prisons upon its prisoners and guards alike?

He added: And then what of our warden or wardens, for whom we have always acted as discrete perceptors?

Brocklebank writes: The true function of cat-fancying being to quiet the mind in order to make it susceptible to divine influences.

Rumrill said: I do not, lest you fret, intend to hand off to you a series of directives as thick as a book, in cramped type, and with a misaligned letter *S*, in the expectation that you will follow these instructions while I am away. Brocklebank's methods, when first he forgot or pretended to forget that Rumrill was a stranger to him, have become, I feel—and feel he would feel as well—obsolete.

He added: If his methods could be said to have been his methods.

Rumrill said: It is quite enough for me to explain to you, as I've done, albeit with aid of these prepared notes, the circumstances in which you find my household and its number of cats, and the thoughts that led to the establishment of said household, and then the new habits that I developed thanks in part to this household; not to forget the ways in which whatever environments I occupied previously formed those same habits that, in turn, faced with a new ecology, caused this household to be disposed as you found it this morning or evening when you stepped out of the weather of the big world into its I think the word is "rarefied" atmosphere. It is enough for us, in fact, to have this intimate interview, to which I have not in fact invited you because there will be any sort of decision made based on your replies to my queries.

He added: I have no queries.

Rumrill said: Whether you might or might not be reliable young citizens insofar as the maintenance of my twenty cats—none of whom have thought it prudent, why I can only guess, to visit us here as we stand, elegant, in our puddles, unsure whether right leg or left should next take the bulk of our civilized weights—is of no great importance at this stage of our relationship. What is important is that I begin with my spiel to inculcate in you the rhythms and the vocabulary and thus thoughts and thus states of mind and thus perceptions and thus behavior I feel will enable you to slough off the assumptions of your previous life and become the ideal caretakers for my shy or perhaps nonexistent but in any case precious fellow residents.

He added: Wherever they may be.

Brocklebank writes: Becoming increasingly aware of how much the planning and execution of an idea depend on, or are influenced by, the individual mode of production.

Rumrill said: There is also the possibility, it would be foolish of you to discount it, that when I say the woman in the stacks left our town and went, perhaps, to Istanbul—there to live a life that to Rumrill was unimaginable save as a version of the life he imagined she must have lived while still resident in our town—that I mean this not literally but to be taken as what is popularly known as a euphemism. A euphemism for what, I cannot say.

He added: Nor shall we speculate.

Rumrill said: There is also the possibility, why not admit it, that when I say that Mr. Brocklebank burned to death, I mean this to be recognized as another clever usage of a rhetorical device with a Greek name I can't remember, or in any case what is popularly known as "a dirty lie." To what end, I cannot guess.

He added: *Scesis Onomaton*, maybe.

Brocklebank writes: Having the feeling, when it

comes down to it, that it's not necessarily my ears that do my hearing, nor my eyes that do my seeing.

Rumrill said: Where will I be while you are left here with my cats? Surely you've guessed that I too would go to Istanbul.

He added: Or "Istanbul."

Brocklebank writes: In any case the circumstances for taking action are in my case different from yours.

Rumrill said: When you look out of that uncharred picture window, that rectangle in my study, you'll see a polygon of sky that has drawn away from our town in apprehension. I suspect it will only get farther in time.

He added: You arrived together.

He added: You'll leave alone.

Brocklebank writes: Taking this as a guide and continuing in like manner.

Sources: Peter Ablinger, Robert Ashley, Milton Babbitt, John Bender, Anthony Braxton, Earle Brown, Ferruccio Busoni, John Cage, Cornelius Cardew, Ornette Coleman, György Kurtág, Bill Dixon, Julius Eastman, Morton Feldman, Henry Flynt, Kyle Gann, Gérard Grisey, Lejaren Hiller, James Gibbons Huneker, Charles Ives, Tom Johnson, Ben Johnston, Rolf Julius, Mauricio Kagel, Gottfried Michael Koenig, Ernst Krenek, Joan La Barbara, Elodie Lauten, György Ligeti, Alvin Lucier, Walter Marchetti, Phill Niblock, Nam June Paik, Harry Partch, Pauline Oliveros, Steve Reich, Roger Reynolds, Arnold Schoenberg, Allen Shawn, Karlheinz Stockhausen, Lois Svard, Giancarlo Toniutti, Stefan Wolpe, La Monte Young.

Chicago/Champaign, 2008–2012

JEREMY M. DAVIES is the author of the novel *Rose Alley* (Counterpath Press) and is senior editor at Dalkey Archive Press.

ellipsis
• • •
press